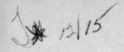

Dante watched her walk across the room, putting as much distance between them as she politely could.

His eyes devoured her. No other woman could make him feel this way—as if he was risking everything—his place on the team, his friendship with Luc, his sanity—just by being in the same room as her. He felt a spike of jealousy as he wondered who had held her since that night? Who had heard her scream with pleasure? Who knew that if they stroked Karina from the nape of her neck to the small of her back, she would whimper with need and raise her hips, inviting even more intimate touches? Who had tasted her innocence since he had basked in it?

*Welcome to the hot, sultry and successful
world of Brazilian polo!*

Get ready to spend many

Hot Brazilian Nights!

with Brazil's sexiest polo champions!

Forget privilege and prestige,
this is Gaucho Polo—hard, hot and unforgiving...
like the men who play the game!

Off the field, the Thunderbolts are
notorious heartbreakers, but what happens
when they meet the one person
who can tame that unbridled passion?

You may have already met
gorgeous team captain Gabe in

Christmas Nights with the Polo Player

Now get ready to meet the rest of the team in

In the Brazilian's Debt
March 2015

At the Brazilian's Command
April 2015

Brazilian's Nine Months' Notice
November 2015

Back in the Brazilian's Bed
December 2015

Available from Harlequin.com
Or visit the author's website:
susanstephens.com/thunderbolt

Susan Stephens

Back in the Brazilian's Bed

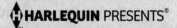

HARLEQUIN PRESENTS®

ISBN-13: 978-0-373-13396-3

Back in the Brazilian's Bed

First North American Publication 2015

Copyright © 2015 by Susan Stephens

Recycling programs
for this product may
not exist in your area.

The publisher acknowledges the copyright holder
of the additional work:

Christmas at The Chatsfield
Copyright © 2015 by Harlequin Books S.A.

Special thanks and acknowledgment are given to Maisey Yates
for her contribution to The Chatsfield series.

Printed in U.S.A.

™ www.Harlequin.com

Susan Stephens was a professional singer before meeting her husband on the Mediterranean island of Malta. In true Harlequin Presents style they met on Monday, became engaged on Friday and married three months later. Susan enjoys entertaining, travel and going to the theater. To relax she reads, cooks and plays the piano, and when she's had enough of relaxing she throws herself off mountains on skis, or gallops through the countryside singing loudly.

Books by Susan Stephens

Harlequin Presents

Master of the Desert
Italian Boss, Proud Miss Prim

Hot Brazilian Nights!

In the Brazilian's Debt
At the Brazilian's Command
Brazilian's Nine Months' Notice

The Skavanga Diamonds

Diamond in the Desert
The Flaw in His Diamond
The Purest of Diamonds?
His Forbidden Diamond

The Acostas!

The Untamed Argentinian
The Shameless Life of Ruiz Acosta
The Argentinian's Solace
A Taste of the Untamed
The Man from Her Wayward Past
Taming the Last Acosta

Visit the Author Profile page
at Harlequin.com for more titles.

For Carly. Welcome back!

CHAPTER ONE

'YOU VOLUNTEERED ME to do *what*?'

Shielding her eyes against the bright morning sun, Karina Marcelos stared at her brother in disbelief. They were standing on the balcony of Luc's eyrie on the penthouse floor of his magnificent cream marble flagship hotel with Rio de Janeiro laid out in front of them. Luc was one crazy polo player—he could be dictatorial when he was in ruling his business empire mode, but he was always considerate of her feelings.

Her brother looked at her with surprise. 'Why the fuss? You're the obvious choice. The job of events organiser for the polo cup couldn't be awarded to anyone better than my highly qualified sister.' With a shrug he left her clenching and unclenching suddenly clammy fists.

She followed him in. 'You'll have to *un*-volunteer me,' she said firmly.

Luc scowled as he sat heavily at his desk. He wasn't used to being denied anything, unless his beloved wife Emma was in the picture.

'I mean it, Luc,' Karina insisted. 'My schedule's packed. I could only give the project a couple of weeks and it's going to need a lot more time than that.'

She could make the time. She could make the event

fly, but that wasn't the reason she was shying away from this plum of a job.

'Too late,' Luc said flatly. 'The posters have gone out and your name's on them. I didn't expect you to kick up a fuss. When I put your name forward to the team, they nearly bit my hand off.'

By team, Luc meant Team Thunderbolt, the world's most infamous gaucho polo players. Luc was a mainstay of the team and so was Dante Baracca, Karina's nemesis. This year it was Dante's turn to host the Gaucho Cup.

'What's wrong now?' her brother demanded, glancing up impatiently from his paperwork.

Where to begin? She didn't want to arouse Luc's suspicions, and finding a plausible excuse not to work with Dante wouldn't be easy. Nor would handling the whisper of awareness that skittered over her skin at the thought of being close to Dante again.

'I need you to do this for me, Karina.'

'I do know what this event means to you, but there are other events organisers.'

'None as good as you,' Luc insisted. 'There's no one who understands the world we work in better than you.'

Karina's glance landed on the cabinet where Luc kept his trophies. He'd left a space for this year's prize. Right next to it, in a pointed reminder that it would be hard, if not impossible to get out of this, there was a trophy belonging to Karina. The International Association of Events Planners had awarded it to her for exceptional merit, and Luc was as proud of that trophy as he was of his own gleaming cups.

'I need you to give me an answer, Karina,' Luc pressed.

'And I need time to think,' she countered.

'What's there to think about?' Settling back in his

chair, Luc pushed his papers to one side. 'Planning the polo cup is easily the most prestigious work you've ever been asked to do, so what's your real problem, Karina?'

She loved her brother dearly, but Luc had no idea what he was asking. She had avoided face-to-face confrontations with Dante for a very good reason—the man was a hundred per cent ice-cold arrogance. She'd avoided him at polo matches, had been forced into his company when Luc and Emma had got together, but apart from that she was always careful to keep her distance from him. If she accepted this commission her avoidance tactics where Dante Baracca was concerned would be shot to hell.

'You should at least have consulted me before you went ahead with this.'

'My apologies,' Luc mocked, gesturing widely to express his frustration. 'I can't imagine why I thought you'd be thrilled. You're the go-to events organiser in Rio, Karina,' he reminded her tensely. 'Who else am I going to ask?'

Her brother was right in that arranging the fixture would be an exciting challenge. It was just the man she had to deal with that was the problem.

'Dante Baracca is an arrogant, humourless dictator,' she murmured, speaking her thoughts out loud.

'He's a powerful, successful man,' her brother argued.

'Didn't I just say that?'

Black eyes flashed as the Marcelos siblings stared each other out.

Karina didn't want to upset her brother, but Luc was equally determined that she would take the job.

'What aren't you telling me?' he demanded shrewdly.

Ice slid down her spine.

'There has to be something,' he insisted. 'We've known

Dante for years. I play on the same team. I'd know if there was a problem. I hope you don't believe his press?'

'He doesn't intimidate me, if that's what you think. And as for his reputation…' She blew out a contemptuous breath. 'Dante's the devil incarnate if you listen to the media—and much as I would love to take on the challenge of working with someone like that, I would have thought that my brother, of all people, would do me the courtesy of allowing me to refuse this job.'

Luc shook his head. 'No can do, Karina. Too much money has been invested in publicity for you to pull out now.' He gave her the look that had melted a thousand hearts. 'Do this one thing for me and I'll never ask again.'

She smiled thinly. 'Until the next time?'

'I've never known you to be so unreasonable.'

She shared a lot with him, but not everything. 'I'll sort something out,' she promised.

'There's nothing to sort out,' Luc insisted. 'We want you. Dante wants you.'

Somehow, she doubted that.

Her mind was already racing. If the posters had gone out, she would have to have a banner added, announcing her replacement. It would have to be someone good—someone who was trusted by the polo community. She might not want the job, but she would do everything she could to make sure things went well for Luc and his team. She would still be cheering for them.

'If it's Dante private life worrying you, it's none of our concern. And he won't have time to notice you in that sense as he'll have so many admirers around him.'

'Thanks for the reassurance,' she said dryly. Luc was right in that there were always polo groupies hanging round the players, and she had never been the glamorous type, let alone wanted to compete with them.

'You're my sister,' Luc pointed out now with exasperation, as if that were enough in itself to disqualify her from attracting male attention. 'Dante will only want to do business with you. I hope you've got more sense than to think anything else?'

'Of course. What do you take me for?'

'A highly successful and very beautiful woman, who could never think of Dante Baracca as anything more than a childhood friend and my teammate.'

'And a man to avoid,' she murmured beneath her breath.

'What was that?' Luc asked suspiciously.

'I don't have to like all your teammates.'

'You don't have to take an unreasonable dislike to them either. Sign the contract, Karina. I'm done waiting.'

And throw herself across Dante's path again—work with him on a daily basis?

It had been a long time since she'd been the tomboy tagging along with her brother's gang, sharing a prickly if somewhat reluctant acceptance from his friends. But she should do this for Luc. He'd done so much for her. He'd brought her up single-handed when their parents had died. There was just one fly in that ointment. Luc had done a brilliant job but had often been distracted, which had given Karina all the time she had needed to get into mischief and more.

As Luc uncapped his pen she was forced to accept the fact that her brother meant more to her than her own stubborn pride. She would just have to put the past behind her, as they had told her to do in the hospital. She would lift up her head and move forward. Dealing with

Dante Baracaa was not beyond her. And she'd put a good face on it. Luc deserved nothing less.

'I should thank you for putting my name forward,' she admitted as she stepped forward to sign the contract.

Luc laughed with relief. 'Everyone wanted you—and if I hadn't suggested you, I think you'd have cut me off at the knees.'

'Maybe.' Angling her chin, she gave her brother an affectionate grin. At least one of them was happy. And she would be a fool to turn this down. This wasn't just the most prestigious job to come her way, it was *the* job.

Luc came around the desk to give her a hug. 'All that fuss about nothing. This is going to be the best thing you've ever done.'

Dante Baracca was *not* a fuss about nothing. Hiding her concerns, she returned Luc's hug. Stepping back, she assessed one of the most striking men in polo. All the players on Team Thunderbolt were forces to be reckoned with, and her brother Luc was no exception. She made allowances for his dictatorial side. He tolerated her constant challenges. They loved each other, and of course she'd do this for him, regardless of the consequences.

'I know Dante used to provoke the hell out of you when you were young,' Luc remarked as he relaxed into his triumph. 'No one was more surprised than me when you practically made him guest of honour at your eighteenth birthday party.'

Karina flinched as she remembered and had to pin a smile to her face. 'My friends wanted him there.' She shrugged. 'And there's been a lot of water under the bridge since then.' Monumental understatement.

Unaware of the undercurrents, Luc laughed off her comment. 'If you say so. I haven't seen you anywhere near Dante since that night, so I'm guessing he said something out of turn, but whatever he did to upset you, my advice is to leave it in the past so you can see the bigger picture.'

She could see the bigger picture and it wasn't pretty.

Turning away, she walked to the window to put some distance between herself and her sharp-eyed brother.

'Dante is the lynchpin of our team,' he stressed. 'He's hosting the polo cup. We need someone to organise it. What more do you need to know?'

'Nothing,' she agreed, staring blindly out of the window.

Karina would be the first to admit she'd been a wild child. Dante had been a big part of that past, but while he'd been worldly and experienced, she'd taken longer to grow up. She'd been naïve and a bit of a dreamer, and had paid a high price for her lack of sophistication. Growing up fast had been forced on her. Putting her sensible head on had come too late. She had clipped her party wings, but it still tore her up to know that by then the damage had been done. It had been a steep learning curve ever since, and that had been something in which Dante had played no part...

'I understand this is the biggest contract you've ever handled,' Luc remarked, misreading her preoccupation. 'You're bound to have concerns, Karina, but I know you can nail this.'

'I'll do a good job for you,' she promised, turning to face him.'

'I know you will. That's why I want you and no one else to handle this contract. And, believe me,' Luc added with a smile to reassure her, 'no one finds Dante easy.'

'With the possible exception of the women in his life,' she countered dryly.

'What's that to you?' Luc said suspiciously.

'Absolutely nothing.' She held his stare steadily until he looked away.

Leaning back against the cold, smooth glass, she remembered begging Luc to let her continue her studies abroad. She'd given him the excuse that she'd had enough of Rio and being under his wing, and that it was time for her to make her own way in life. Luc hadn't guessed for a minute that all she'd really wanted was to get away from Dante. Luc had paid for her to go to catering college, which had turned out better than she had expected. She'd ended up winning a full scholarship to a prestigious Swiss training facility for event planners, where she had excelled. Equipped with an honours diploma, she had returned to Rio ready to change the world—or, at least, her brother's hotel chain—only to find a highly sceptical Luc waiting for her.

She had won her spurs by working on small assignments for him, until he'd finally allowed her to work on his bigger projects. This Gaucho Polo Cup was the biggest project to date by far. And, yes, she wanted to be part of it. And, yes, she knew she could make it a success. She had the expertise and the inside knowledge when it came to the world of polo. But she'd be working with Dante, and that was a problem. She wasn't the person she'd been in the past, but would Dante see that? According to the press he hadn't changed and the word 'wild' still defined him. She only had to open a magazine to see him dating another woman. Dante Baracca attracted glamorous females in dizzying succession, but then he discarded them twice as fast. So nothing had changed.

'Dante Baracca, the hard man of polo.' Her brother said this with amusement, quoting a phrase most often associated with his teammate. 'You'll be the envy of half the women in the world.'

'Half the women in the world don't need a wake-up call from me,' she argued. 'And, if they did, I'd tell them that their idol has feet of clay.'

Luc drew back his head to give her a look. 'That's a little harsh when you've barely spoken to the man for years.'

'For a very good reason,' she dismissed. 'Who needs trouble like Dante Baracca in their life?'

Dante could be charming when it suited him, but he could also be hard and cold. If Dante would behave professionally, she might be able to make this work. If not... Her thoughts took her back to a man with black hair, black eyes and a black heart, a man who looked like a Gypsy king with gold earrings glinting in his ears. She could still remember the night Dante had punched those gold hoops into his own earlobes because she'd challenged him to do so. They'd both been wild when he'd been fourteen and she'd been ten, back in the day when they could take risks and get away with them.

'Stop frowning, Karina. Anyone would think I'd hooked you up with a monster. Here...' Luc held out a magazine, which he obviously intended to reassure her. 'Take a look at this—Dante's riding the crest of the wave at the moment.'

Dante Baracca was on the front cover. Of course he was. Where else would the god of the game be?

'There couldn't be a better time for you two to be getting together.'

'We won't be *getting together*,' she insisted. 'I'll be working alongside him.'

'Of course you will,' Luc agreed—to placate her, she suspected.

She made herself stare at the photograph while Luc looked on with approval.

Thank goodness Luc couldn't hear her heart thundering at the sight of a man who had always affected her profoundly, both for good and for bad. The photo showed Dante seated bareback on a horse at sunset on the fringes of the surf. He was stripped to the waist with his face in profile. His powerful torso was warmed to a seductive bronze by the mellow rays of the setting sun. He was a daunting sight. The shadows pointed up the harsh angles of his face and delineated his formidable muscles. She had no doubt the photographer's intention had been to big up the legend that was Dante Baracca, and in that he had succeeded.

Dante had more tattoos than she remembered. All the members of Luc's team had a Thunderbolt inked on their torsos, but it wouldn't have surprised her to learn that these new additions to Dante's hard frame had been handcrafted by the devil.

Her mouth dried as she thought back. She would never shake the past. In many ways she didn't want to. The memories were bittersweet. The loss had been too great, the sadness too searing, and Dante would always be part of that. He was still wearing the earrings that matched her own. Dante had given them to her on her eighteenth birthday—teasing her, saying they could be twins, but the look in his eyes had not been that of a sibling, and the earrings had been pushed to the back of a drawer after the party, because they'd become too cruel a reminder of Dante and everything he stood for…too close a reminder of kindred spirits who had almost destroyed each other.

'Stop fretting, Karina,' Luc coaxed when she frowned. 'You can handle one barbarian. Why not two?'

'If Dante is prepared to do things my way, it might work,' she mused distractedly.

'That should be fun to watch,' Luc commented dryly.

'This is no joke, Lucas.'

'Clearly, as you're calling me by my Sunday name.'

'I mean it,' she said, rounding on her brother. 'My work is a serious business. You and Dante may have grown up wild on the pampas—'

'As did you,' Luc cut in, his tone turning hard. 'What's wrong with you, Karina? You never used to be like this. Just because you're about to do business with a man women lust after doesn't mean you have to wear a hair shirt. You can loosen up and make this project a success, or you can carry this ridiculous grudge you seem to have against Dante to its ultimate conclusion and wreck the match.'

'Okay,' she said, holding up her hands. 'Just so long as we get one thing clear. You can't just hire me out to your friends whenever you feel like it without my permission. No more Dante Baraccas—okay?'

Luc turned to face the door where his secretary was miming an apology for the interruption. 'Why don't you tell Dante that yourself? Come in, my friend...'

Striding forward to greet his fellow polo player, Luc added, 'Karina can't wait to tell you what she has planned.'

CHAPTER TWO

TIME HALTED AS they stared at each other. Dante's body reacted instantly as the past flooded back—a past best forgotten while her brother was in the room. He hadn't seen Karina this close since the night of her eighteenth birthday, when he'd seen her in infinitely more detail than he was seeing her now.

'Come in, my friend—come in.'

He broke eye contact with Karina as Luc drew him deeper into the room, but the aftershock of his feelings for her blanked out everything but Karina. The strength of those feelings made him wonder if his first impulse had been correct. He'd been strongly tempted to veto Luc's suggestion when Karina's name had been suggested to the team. Why resurrect the past? He didn't need that sort of trouble in his life. Karina had been wild, as had he, and though he'd heard how successful she had become, he had no proof that she'd changed.

In the end he had decided that vetoing Karina on the strength of evidence from the past was mean-minded of him, and that as the sister of a teammate he should at least give her a chance. He had already made plans to keep contact between them to a minimum while she was working on his ranch. She'd avoided him for many years, so he was confident that that was what she would want too. But now, being in the same room as Karina, he was forced to rethink. Her effect on him was profound. He understood now why no other woman had ever matched up to her. But all the old reasons for resisting Karina remained. He was a player in life as well as on the field, and as the sister of his teammate Karina Marcelos was forbidden fruit.

'Dante...'

Her voice was soft and polite—for her brother's sake, he suspected, as the expression in her eyes was at odds with that professional exterior as she crossed the room to greet him. There was no intimacy at all in her gaze. Intimacy? She was almost hostile towards him. Had that single night all those years ago taken such a toll? Apparently, it had. There was nothing to be done about it. Karina had wanted more from him than he'd been able to give. He had thrown her out of his bed for the best of reasons. He had nothing to give her in the emotional sense, and still marvelled that he had put his concern for Karina above his own selfish lust. He'd been utterly selfish back then.

He was still where women were concerned, he reflected as her cool gaze levelled on his. He still had nothing to offer. The only difference today was the fact that she wasn't interested. Worse. The light had gone from her eyes. Where was the Karina he had known? What had happened to the tomboy who would give him as good as she got?

'You look well,' he said, still searching for clues.

'Do I?'

His groin tightened at the challenge. She wasn't so dead inside after all. She had always been a good actress, and he could understand why she was cool with him. The blow to her pride must have been immense. Saving her from him had come at a heavy price. Their friendship was dead.

'You look well, Dante.'

'Thank you.'

The polite exchange over, he returned to assessing Karina. She was all woman now, not a girl to provoke and tease. Her figure had filled out and her thick black hair gleamed with good health, though since that night she had started tying it back severely. Whenever he caught a glimpse of her at a polo match, it was dragged back, and it was dragged back today—so different from the past when it had cascaded in wild tangles down her back. They had both changed. They were both very different people now. He had responsibilities, while Karina's career had obviously grounded her, and though that reassured him on a professional level, this was not the girl he had vowed to stay away from for her own good but a woman who would keep him at bay.

'Can I get you something to drink?' she asked politely.

Hemlock, her eyes suggested, which made him force back a smile. 'Just water, please.'

Her expression gave nothing away as she turned to do the honours, but when she returned and gave him the glass and their fingers brushed, her cheeks pinked up betrayingly. She could act all she liked, but she still felt the connection between them, just as he did.

His hunting instinct rose and swirled around them. Sensing this, she shot him a warning glance. She hadn't forgiven him for kicking her out of his bed. He couldn't blame her when he hadn't bothered with explanations. A prior, pressing appointment had done the job. If she'd stayed they would have destroyed each other. She'd been too young, too innocent for him. Progressing their friendship into something more than one night had been a car crash waiting to happen, but all Karina had seen was his betrayal.

His eyes devoured her as she crossed the room. It amused him to think that she was putting as much distance between them as she could, when at one time she would have stayed to plague and tease him. No other woman made him feel this way, as if he was risking everything—his place on the team, his friendship with Luc—his very sanity, just by being in the same room as her. And then jealousy swamped him. Who had held her since that night? Who had heard Karina scream with pleasure? Who knew that if they stroked her from the nape of her neck to the small of her back she would whimper with need and raise her hips, inviting even more intimate touches? Who had tasted her innocence since that night?

'It's so good to have you here, Dante.'

He shot into fully alert mode as her brother spoke to him. Luc had an easy manner with his teammates and as he crossed the room to put an arm around Dante, it was in complete contrast to the tension between Dante and Luc's sister. He had to put all thoughts of Karina aside before he could respond to his friend. 'Thank you, Luc. It's good to be here.'

And then they were talking about the match and their latest pony acquisitions, but all the time he was aware of Karina. He'd ridden with her brother since they'd been boys. Luc and he were brothers in arms, both fiercely competitive, and he had never once discussed Karina with her brother. A man's sister was inviolable, and though for years he had burned to know if Karina had a lover, it had been a question he would never ask Luc.

'Karina has signed the contract!'

'Excellent.' He swung around to face her after her brother's announcement. 'There's no one I can think of who is better qualified to organise the Gaucho Cup.'

'No one understands the demands of polo players better than my sister,' Luc confirmed warmly.

Karina said nothing.

Luc, who appeared not to have noticed his sister bristling, stared at the water in Dante's glass. 'Are you sure you wouldn't like something stronger?'

'I'm certain, thank you. I want to keep a clear head.'

Karina's stare sharpened on his face.

'Shall we?' she said, glancing towards the boardroom table.

'Certainly.' He walked across the room to hold her chair for her.

Karina proved her worth within minutes, picking up points his lawyers had missed. He should have felt completely confident in her abilities, but found himself disappointed instead. Knowing Karina as he had, he had anticipated something extra, a little dose of magic that would have lifted the event above the norm. Her initial thoughts were well thought through, considering she'd only just signed the contract, and he had no doubt those plans would be executed flawlessly, but her ideas lacked oomph. They were pedestrian and he had expected more of her.

'Well, I think that's it,' she said when her thoughts were exhausted. 'I hope you have a pleasant journey home.'

He had intended to leave immediately after the meeting, but now he was determined to stay. He wanted to get to the bottom of the changes in Karina and to make a final decision as to whether or not she could realise the vision he had for the polo event. From what he'd seen so far, he had some doubts. Smiling easily, he relaxed back. 'I'm in no hurry.'

Her expression hardened. He raised a brow. Her brother, once again, remained oblivious to the undercurrents between them. In fact, it was Luc who rescued the situation, saying, 'You're not leaving yet, surely?'

He smiled back at Luc. 'No, of course not.'

'Karina,' Luc chastised her when she remained silent and still. 'Are you forgetting your manners completely? Dante can't leave yet. This calls for champagne.'

He added his support to Luc's suggestion. 'I agree with Luc. What's the rush?'

The look Karina gave him called for more hemlock.

She clearly didn't want him to stay, which made him wonder why she was feeling quite so defensive and angry. Could she have held a grudge for so long? Apparently, she could—but there was one interesting fact: she might be looking at him as if he were the devil, but not a devil she wanted to run from, rather a devil she wanted to stay and fight. That was a great improvement. It fired her up— turned her from an expressionless automaton into the Karina he had known.

'You're the client. Whatever suits you,' she said, smiling a plastic smile.

Hard eyes. Hard mouth. Hard man. How could she ever have imagined she could work with Dante? He couldn't know, of course, that what they'd done had set in motion a train of events that would have such far-reaching repercussions. She had to remind herself that the past had no part to play in these business discussions. She was proud of the career she'd built up. She'd worked hard for it, and would allow nothing and no one to take it from her—not even Dante Baracca. She'd give him no cause for complaint. If there was one thing she'd learned while working for her brother, it was that a woman had to be twice as strong as any man in the workplace, and that emotion had no part to play.

'Your sister seems preoccupied,' Dante remarked to Luc, as if she'd left the room. 'Do you think she will find it impossible to work with me?'

'I think she can handle you,' Luc said dryly.

She swung around to confront them both. 'I'm still in the room. If you expect me to run this project for you, please don't discuss me as if I'm a blotter on my brother's desk.'

Dante's wry glance look suggested she had fallen into his trap. He had meant to provoke her to draw her back into the conversation.

'Please excuse my sister,' Luc joked. 'You remember what she's like, don't you, Dante? But there's one thing I can assure you, she's very good at her job.'

'I'm sure she is,' Dante agreed, with a look that made her cheeks burn.

'Well… If you will both excuse me?'

Karina stiffened as Luc started collecting up his things.

'I've got another appointment I simple can't miss.'

You can't leave me!

Ignoring the look she gave him, her brother did just that.

Clever Luc. He'd left her with no alternative but to stay and entertain their guest.

Dante broke the silence first. 'Well, Miss Prim.' His voice was low and amused. 'Why are you so reluctant to work with me?'

She drew herself up. 'I don't know what makes you say that. I'm looking forward to this project immensely.'

'Liar,' Dante murmured.

He sucked the breath from her lungs with that single word.

'Are you still hurting after that night?'

Shock coursed through her. She couldn't believe what he'd just said. 'My *only* interest is to organise the best event the polo world has ever seen.'

'Worthy and dull?' he flashed.

Her cheeks blazed red under this attack. Was that was how she'd come across? When her brother left the room, she had been expecting a few pleasantries, and then the chance to make another appointment to see Dante to discuss her plans—and only that.

'I expected more of you, Karina.' His tone was scathing.

Completely thrown, she went into defensive mode. 'I'll give you my best. My clients have never been disappointed. My past record speaks for itself.'

'Maybe your previous clients haven't been as demanding as me.'

She couldn't believe he was being so aggressive and, unsettled, she looked away. Reaching out, he cupped her chin and brought her back so she had nowhere to look but into his eyes. 'Why so defensive, Karina?' he goaded. 'What aren't you telling me?'

'I don't know what you mean. You're a valued client, and I never break my promise to a client. That should be enough for you.'

Dante's eyes narrowed. 'You haven't answered my question.'

Nor would she. Shaking him off, she stepped back. 'If we're going to do business together—'

'You will have to lighten up,' he supplied, in a tone that spoke worryingly of Dante's growing doubt that she was up to the task.

She had to remind herself how many difficult clients she'd had in the past, and that Dante was just one more. But though she had always succeeded in winning clients over in the past, Dante was a unique case, and the way he was looking at her now, as if he wanted her to defend herself...

'If you don't like my suggestions—'

He cut her off with a laugh. 'Brava, Karina. I had begun to think there was nothing left of the wildcat I remember.'

There wasn't anything left of that reckless young woman. Was he suggesting she had learned nothing since that night?

'You accepted this assignment because you can't resist it,' he accused her, bringing his face close. 'How do I know this?' With a shrug he stood back. 'You accepted this contract because you won't let your brother down. And you won't let yourself down because you have far too much pride.'

'I have pride?' she demanded on an incredulous laugh.

'Honoured client?' Dante reminded her, easing onto one hip.

She would come to regret those words, Karina suspected as she looked away.

'My driver is waiting downstairs.'

She stared at him blankly.

'You're coming with me.'

She shook her head. 'I have work to do.'

'Yes,' Dante agreed. 'My work. My contract that you just signed.'

'Seriously, I really don't have time for this.'

'Then make time,' he said coldly, reminding her of just how harsh he could be. 'I can't do business with you while you're tense like this.'

'Tense? I'm just busy, Dante. I only wish I could leave,' she lied, softening her tone in the hope of placating him, 'But, unfortunately, I have a very busy day ahead of me.'

'With important clients?'

He knew there was no client more important than he was, and the air was electric between them. Two wills colliding and neither one of them prepared to back down. But Dante had the better of her today because he knew she wouldn't let her brother down.

'This trip?' she prompted. 'What did you have in mind?'

'Let's get out of here and then I'll tell you.' Dante held the door for her, and as she walked through he murmured, 'One thing you will discover about me, *chica*, is that I never do anything without a very good reason.'

She stopped dead right in front of him. 'Let's get one thing clear from the start. I am not your *chica*.'

Instead of taking offence, Dante stepped up close. He stood so close, looking down at her, that she could see the tiger gold in his eyes. She held his blazing gaze steadily, though her stomach was coiled in a knot.

'What are you frightened of, Karina?' he murmured in a voice she knew so well.

A quiver of awareness rippled across her shoulders even as she stood up to him. 'Not you, that's for sure. Shall we go?' she said.

'You're very confident that I won't take my business elsewhere,' he said as they walked along the corridor side by side. 'Why is that, Karina?'

'You're not a fool?' she said.

Dante's husky laugh ran a full-blown shiver of arousal down her spine. His laugh was so familiar, too familiar. Dante had always possessed an animal energy that attracted her, however hard she tried to fight it off. And he had always understood her as no one else could. He probably knew that right now every part of her was on full alert just being close to him. After that night she had wondered if she would ever be capable of feeling anything for anyone again. She had also wondered if the connection between them would fade across the years. She knew now that neither one of those suspicious was true. If anything, she was more aware of him.

She had to forget the past if she was going to do business with Dante. She would have to forget everything, just as he must accept that everything in her life had changed.

'You never married?' he queried out of the blue as they stepped into the empty elevator.

She looked at him, shocked that he could ask such a personal question, then remembered that Dante had always been known for speaking his mind.

'Neither did you,' she countered. Fixing her stare on the illuminated floor numbers as they flashed on and off, she tried not to respond when he shrugged and smiled faintly.

'I've been too busy, Karina. What's your excuse?'

'Do I need one?'

She spoke mildly, but there was the faintest of threats

in her voice. *Leave it, Dante,* came over loud and clear. He loved it when Karina came back to life. He loved to see fire flashing in her eyes as it once had. Every woman seemed pallid to him by comparison with Karina—until he had walked into her brother's office this morning and wondered if there was any of her old spirit left. There was, and there was more for him to tease out, he suspected, though she stood as far away from him as possible in the elevator. When the door slid open and she walked out ahead of him, she didn't speak a word as they headed for his limousine. Perhaps she didn't trust herself to speak.

His driver opened the door for them, and she got in. She remained silent at his side, allowing him plenty of time to weigh up the shadows in her eyes.

'You haven't told me where we're going yet,' she reminded him, conscious of his scrutiny.

'You always used to like surprises, Karina.'

'And now I don't have time for them.' She crossed her legs and sat up primly to make her point. 'I have a working life to consider,' she added, when he continued to stare at her.

'Then stop worrying, because the place I'm taking you is directly connected to the business between us.

'Relax,' he advised.

'I'm perfectly relaxed,' she snapped, staring straight ahead.

Dante's driver drove carefully through the crowded streets. It was carnival. How could she have forgotten? The city was packed with musicians and performers, and crowds from all over the world. At one time this had been her favourite event of the year.

'You used to love carnival,' Dante commented, as if he had picked up on her thoughts. 'Has that changed now?'

'It hasn't changed.' She felt a charge as she turned to look at him. His hands, his lips, his face, his body all so familiar, were within a few scant inches of her, and her mouth dried as she turned to look out of the window at the exuberant crowd. Carnival was all about rhythm and music, abandonment and lust, and here she was, old before her time, dressed in a sober business suit, feeling like a dried-up leaf.

'I'm not dressed for this,' she murmured, unconsciously voicing her inner concerns.

'I don't know what you're worried about,' Dante argued as his driver parked. 'Who cares what you're wearing? It's the spirit of carnival that counts.'

That was what worried her. She'd used to have plenty of spirit, but life changed you.

'I can't—these heels…'

Dante glanced at her feet and laughed. 'That's the worst excuse I ever heard.'

She shook her head in disagreement. 'We can't afford to waste time here when we could be discussing plans for the polo cup.'

'That's precisely why we're here,' he argued, reaching for the door handle. 'The event will be a huge success— if you can relax enough to organise it.'

'I can relax,' she insisted, pressing back against the seat. 'I just don't have a lot of time. I thought you understood that.'

'I understand that you're making excuses,' he said, opening the door and getting out.

What the hell was wrong with Karina? What had happened to her sense of humour—her sense of fun? At one time it wouldn't have been she leading him astray and distracting him from his work. In the past it hadn't been possible to keep Karina away from carnival, but now it seemed she hadn't even registered the fact that that it was carnival week in Rio. She'd be no use in this sombre mood to the event he wanted to create. He had expected the Karina he'd once known, would come up with something fabulous, something that would appeal to all ages. 'Shall we?' he invited, helping her out of the car—or rather drawing her out, as she seemed so reluctant. He was beginning to wonder if he'd made a huge mistake to allow Luc to talk him into this.

'Lead the way,' she said, with the same lack of enthusiasm, as if he hadn't touched her at all.

He intended to lead. He intended to elicit a reaction from her. When they had all been kids together the annual carnival had been the highlight of their year, and that was exactly what he wanted to re-create on his ranch for the Gaucho Cup.

'All work and no play will destroy your creative juices,' he warned, as she stared around.

'If you say so.'

Her small smile was better than nothing at all, he supposed.

'We need to get a move on, Karina,' he prompted. 'The procession will start any time now.'

'Okay.'

Wobbling on the cobbles in her high-heeled shoes, she did look out of place—as she so obviously felt. His stone heart responded just a little. Even back when Karina had been a tomboy, tormenting the life out of him, he'd cared about her in his offhand teenage way. He still cared about her, and felt compelled to get to the bottom of the changes in someone who had used to shed light, but who now cast only shadows.

CHAPTER THREE

IGNORING DANTE'S OFFER to link arms, she walked ahead. This wasn't a personal expedition, this was business.

Really?

Dante didn't need to know that just being within touching distance of him made her heart go crazy, or that she beginning to feel the excitement of carnival thaw the ice around her heart. She hadn't done this for ages—walked in the city for no better reason than to have fun. She hadn't felt this free for years. Her gaze was darting around like a hermit let out of a cave as she desperately tried to soak up all the sights and sounds and smells at once.

She felt drunk on them, elated, after the hushed silence of her brother's luxury hotel, and for a moment she was so wrapped up in events around her that she stopped walking altogether and got jostled along by the crowd. She almost lost her balance and then a steadying hand rescued her—Dante's. She sucked in a noisy breath, glad that the ruckus from the crowd drowned it out. Even that briefest of touches was a warning of how receptive she still was to Dante.

She shouldn't have come here with him, she fretted as she made for some shadows beneath the awning of a shop. Carnival in Rio was the highest-octane party in the world. No one came to carnival to discuss dry business deals or to cement business relationships. If couples talked at all, their faces were close and their eyes were locked on each other.

The music, the colour, the spectacle, the noise, the heat of the sun and the warmth of the cobbled street beneath her feet, combined with the scent of cinnamon and spices, made a riotous feast for the senses, and she had been on an austere diet. Appealing to her senses was the very last thing on her agenda for today. Logic and facts were all she needed to make the Gaucho Cup a success.

But she was here. *And* with him. *Get over it. Get out there and make the most of it.*

'Hold on,' Dante cautioned, as she followed a sudden impulse to plunge into the crowd. 'It gets wild from here.'

Like she didn't know that—though anything was wild compared to the way she'd been living. She exulted in the beat of the approaching drums as they grew louder. Maybe she wasn't so dead inside after all. She wasn't— she wasn't dead at all. In fact, she had to fight the urge to go along the crowd and lose herself in the echo of a different life.

'Karina!'

Dante's shout brought her to her senses just in time. Of course she wouldn't have followed that impulse, and of course she held back. She knew better than to let herself go these days because she knew where that led.

They had reached a small square. The crowd had moved ahead of them, leaving just the two of them on the street. Dante was leaning back against a wall, watching her with a puzzled expression on his face. His forearms were crossed over his powerful chest, and somewhere along the way he'd removed his jacket and tie. However hard she tried to look away, she couldn't, and when she tried desperately hard to blank her mind to the image of a ridiculously good-looking man, she failed there too.

Then she noticed that an elderly couple had stopped to watch them, as if they had somehow created a mini-drama to be played out in silence between them. She quickly dragged her attention from Dante, only to see the old lady wink at her. She wanted to explain that there was nothing between them, but that wouldn't have been very professional of her so she smiled instead. The elderly couple were having such a happy day—why spoil it for them? But if her feelings were so obvious to them, were they obvious to Dante?

He smiled at the old couple too. He could be charming when he wanted. And then the crowd thickened once more and the elderly couple disappeared into the throng, while Dante stood in front of her to protect her as the crowd surged past.

'I can look after myself,' she protested, when he put an arm around her to draw her close.

'Is chivalry out of fashion these days?'

His look was mocking. She responded in kind. 'Chivalry? That's not a word I readily associate with you.'

'Why not?' he demanded, looking at her keenly.

She looked away. She didn't want to get into it. They were here in the middle of carnival with nowhere else to go. She had to make the best of it, and with more than two million people milling about on the streets of Rio it was important to stay close.

The crowd pushed them together as they walked along. Her body tingled each time she touched Dante. It was a distracting client relationship tool, she told herself sternly. Cold emptiness had been her companion for so long she felt each light brush as if it were an intentional touch. And then he was distracted by one of the beautiful young samba dancers and her stomach squeezed tight as she watched them exchange kisses on both cheeks like old friends. She carefully masked her feelings when he came back to her.

'My apologies for not introducing you, Karina.'

She shrugged it off, but Dante wasn't fooled. 'Are you jealous?' he probed with amusement.

'Certainly not. Why would I be?' she demanded, as a little green imp stabbed her with its pitchfork.

Dante's smile broadened infuriatingly as he took her arm to steer her through the crowd. 'We must head for the main square where all the performers are gathering.'

More choice for him?

Whatever Dante did or didn't do with half the girls in Rio was no business of hers. Carnival was full of beautiful women. It was a showcase. *It was Dante's hunting ground.* There wasn't a samba school in the city that wasn't represented, and the samba beauties could swivel their bodies to stunning effect. All the men were transfixed by them, and all the girls played up to the most famous man of all: the infamous Dante Baracca.

She *was* jealous.

She was not!

'Karina...'

'Yes?'

As Dante turned to look at her she was determined he wouldn't see, not by so much as the flicker of an eyelash, that she was affected by him, and more than she could ever have anticipated.

'Stay close,' he advised.

That proved impossible when a gang of young girls mobbed him, and she ended up defending him. They wanted his autograph, and, by the look of it, his clothes. Elbowing her way through the scrum, she spread out her arms in front of Dante. 'Senhor Baracca has an important appointment to keep, but I noticed a television crew around the corner—' Barely were the words out of her mouth when the young girls screamed with excitement and ran off.

Dante was amused. 'When I need a bodyguard I'll know who to call.'

'It will cost you extra,' she warned him dryly, moving on.

Dante was right about things getting wild. The decorated floats had arrived and everyone was excited as they trundled into view. 'Your safety's my responsibility,' he explained, when he yanked her close.

'And you're my honoured client,' she reminded him, pulling away. 'If anyone gets protected here, it's you— and you haven't paid my fee yet,' she said dryly.

He laughed. The first honest, open laugh she'd heard from him so far.

'You're one tough lady.'

'Believe it, Dante. You became my responsibility from the moment I agreed to accompany you to the carnival, and I won't let any harm come to you.'

'And I will allow none to come to you,' he assured her with an intensity that made her blink.

Did the same rule apply these days to the women in his bed?

'I can look after myself,' she repeated, wondering if her treacherous heart could beat its way out of her lying mouth. Having Dante this close made her doubt every-thing—her willpower, her powers of reasoned thought...

His husky laugh put an end to her brief moment of panic. It coincided with some more girls recognising him and crowding round. His black eyes mocked her when they went on their way, and he shrugged as he excused himself. 'They said they knew me.'

'I'm sure they do,' she agreed. 'Please, excuse me if I'm interrupting your congregation in the act of worship.'

He laughed again—a wolf laugh, sharp and faintly threatening. 'You *are* jealous. Why fight it, Karina?'

'May I suggest we move on?' she said coolly.

Another few yards on and a girl dancing on a float called out to Dante. All the men were agog as they stared at her. She was beautiful. Wearing feathers and spar-kles and not much more, it was no wonder Dante was so spoiled when every woman laid it on a plate for him.

Including her, Karina remembered, firming her jaw as Dante swung his arm around her shoulders.

'Sorry,' he said again, with a smile that could melt the stoniest of hearts.

She resisted the temptation to melt at his feet. 'Please, don't worry about me. There are plenty of distractions here that prevent me watching you baste your ego.'

'Ah, Karina,' he growled softly, 'have you forgotten that I'm your honoured client?'

'I have forgotten nothing. We signed a contract,' she reminded him crisply, 'so I've got your business.'

'So you don't need to try?' Dante suggested with an amused look.

'Where business is concerned, I can assure you of my full attention. Where anything else is concerned?' She shrugged.

That was the end of that conversation as they were forced into silence by one of the samba bands marching past. The rhythm was infectious, making it impossible to remain tense. Everyone around them had started dancing. The performers and their supporters had put so much effort into the parade even she allowed herself to respond to their energy. It occurred to her as she started dancing that at one time she would have been up there on a float, dancing along with the best of them.

'This is good, Karina.'

Her glance flashed up to Dante.

'Watch and learn, because this is exactly what I want you to re-create on my ranch.'

'Carnival?' She stared up at him in surprise.

She couldn't help noticing how attractive Dante looked when his lips pressed down in wry agreement. 'I'm not asking for too much, am I?' he probed.

He was asking for the world—and he knew it. Carnival took a year to plan, and she had a matter of weeks.

'After all, I'm paying for the best.'

He shrugged again as he said this, and his tone of voice had changed from coaxing to rather more calculating as he added, 'I'm paying for the best, so I expect the best.'

'Of course,' she agreed, relaxing into this return to business, even as she wondered if it could possibly last. 'The impossible I can do.'

'Miracles might take a little longer?' he suggested. 'You will have to work fast.'

There was no leeway in that statement, and she prided herself on always doing the best job faster than anyone else. Dante had turned away to throw a roll of banknotes onto a passing float, reminding her that all the performers were collecting money for charity. People who often had very little themselves worked hard all year to raise money during the parade, which was what made carnival so special. Locating all the cash she had, she tossed it onto the float. She would never lose sight of what this city had done for her. Working here had saved her. The vitality and the energy of Rio de Janeiro had lifted her, giving her barely enough time to brood or think back.

Until now. Dante would never change, she reflected as another group of dancing girls gathered around him. They were all exquisitely dressed and very beautiful, while Dante appeared like a dark pagan god in their midst. She had never felt more like a dowdy grey sparrow as she waited for him outside the circle of girls. If only she'd taken time to change out of her formal business suit, though something told her that more than the suit would have to go if she was going to do business successfully with Dante. She would have to find some of her missing *joie de vivre*—and stand up to him at every twist and turn.

She gave a start when he turned to look at her. Angling her chin, she made as if to leave. She couldn't find it in her heart to blame the girls for loving Dante when his ridiculously handsome image appeared on every Thunderbolt poster in the city, and he looked even better in the flesh, but she was determined to get on with this research project, rather than indulge his slightest whim.

How was her determination to appear disinterested in Dante as anything other than a client going so far?

Not so well. Dante Baracca was back in her life, whether she wanted him there or not, and now it was up to her to harness the tornado and make it co-operate with her vision of how carnival could be adapted to suit the confines of a ranch.

'I'll make sure we enjoy some quality time together so we can have a proper chat about my plans,' Dante reassured her when he returned to her side.

'My plans will take a little time to formulate,' she responded mildly. Dante had a samba girl hanging from each arm. She made no comment when he shooed the girls away.

'We will discuss my plans shortly,' he said.

'I'm prepared to consider your suggestions,' she said, and emphasised, 'Unless it's your way to pay a dog and bark yourself?'

His mouth curved in a grin. 'This new business partnership should be interesting.'

'Exactly as my brother predicted,' she confirmed, turning away.

'Your brother?'

'Shall we get on? Time is short. We should head for the main square,' she reminded him.

Dante drew her into a doorway as the previous year's samba queen danced past. The noise from the accompanying drums was like thunder, and for a few seconds she was glad to lose herself in someone else's moment, but then the girl stopped to put on a special dance for Dante. A leopard never changed its spots, she mused wryly as Dante tucked a roll of notes into the waistband of the girl's thong.

'Turning into a prude, Karina?'

'Miss Prim?' she threw back at him. She shrugged and smiled as the girl with the flawless body danced on her way. 'You do what you like. It's nothing to do with me.'

'Such a shame,' Dante murmured, his dark glittering eyes staring deep into hers. 'I rather thought you might keep me in line.'

'I think you'd enjoy that too much.'

His lips pressed down. 'You never used to be such a killjoy.'

And he was the reason she'd changed, she thought.

No sooner had she dispensed with this latest salvo from Dante than a good-looking guy stopped in front of her and started dancing. Her first impulse was to smile and move on, but then it occurred to her that if Dante could flirt and tease without restriction, why couldn't she?

She was about to find out, Karina guessed. Judging by the look on Dante's face, what was good for the goose definitely wasn't good for the gander. Then another woman—who, having recognised him, began to dance in front of him—distracted Dante, and with a look in her direction he brought the woman into his arms. Retaliation was one thing, but she had no intention of cosying up to her own partner, and had to content herself with covertly watching Dante prove just how good a man could look when he had been born with the rhythm of Brazil in his veins.

This was carnival where anything was possible. Yes. Dance with the devil and you would get burned, she added silently when Dante brushed against her. She knew he was teasing her deliberately, he always had, but she refused to respond and danced on, though Dante made her partner look like a beardless boy.

CHAPTER FOUR

IT WAS A RELIEF when the band for that particular float moved on and their dance partners drifted away with the rest of the crowd. She had realised by that time that she couldn't play games with Dante because the stakes were just too high.

'Why so tense?' he demanded. 'I brought you here to relax and take everything in. Didn't you enjoy dancing with that boy?'

'That...*boy*?' she queried frowning.

Dante shrugged. 'I noticed you kept your distance from him.'

'Are *you* jealous now?'

His look made her shiver. She'd kept her distance from the youth for a very good reason. She didn't want his hands on her. And he had been no threat, but that didn't matter to Dante. There was still fire between them. Maybe there always would be.

More floats arrived, swamping them in noise, colour and people, and saving her from a potentially awkward moment. The happy smiles made it impossible to remain immune to the spell woven by carnival.

Drummers marched in front of each float, and they set up a sound that reverberated through her, making it hard to keep still. In the end she didn't try, and it was while she was swaying to the rhythm that she carelessly backed into Dante. He grabbed her. His hands closed over her body—over a part of her body she never looked at, never showed to the world, kept hidden from everyone, and especially from him. It didn't matter that her shame was covered by layers of clothing, that awkward stumble was all it took for her eyes to fill with tears.

Jostling through a crowd, looking out for each other, was nothing they hadn't done a dozen times before when they had been younger, but today everything had taken on a deeper significance. It was time to put some distance between them. Baring her soul to Dante was the last thing she wanted to do. She had kept her feelings to herself for too long to break down now.

'Dance?' he suggested, at the worst possible moment. *Dance with him?*

Dante's warm breath caressed her skin as he leaned closer. 'Dance and forget everything but carnival, just as you used to.'

Just as she used to? That wasn't possible. Having Dante's hands on her body wasn't possible.

'If you've forgotten how to dance, maybe you have forgotten how to inject the spirit of carnival into your projects,' Dante suggested with narrowed eyes.

Maybe it was the music of her youth and the fact that Dante was offering to dance with her, but more likely it was the challenge in his eyes that pressed her into doing something she had shrunk from for too long. She let herself go. Kicking off her high-heeled shoes, she took one step and then another, and soon she was dancing on the warm, dusty streets of Rio.

Raising her arms, she swayed in time to the music,

allowing the rhythm to dictate her movement. The beat was repetitive and sexy, and her hips seemed to move of their own volition. Closing her eyes, she gave herself up to the music and the sunshine. It was so easy to dance once she'd started, so easy to forget so that all she felt was the urge to live and love and laugh again, and not care about tomorrow...

Which was exactly what had got her into trouble in the first place, she remembered, sobering up fast. 'I think we should go now.' Straightening her suit jacket, she dipped down to pick up her shoes.

'We can't go. Not yet,' Dante ruled. 'This year's samba queen hasn't been crowned and it would be rude to leave before that.'

'People will notice if we're not there?' She turned to give him a sceptical look and then remembered she was talking to Dante Baracca. Dante had been spotted several times by performers on the floats, and his absence at the crowning would definitely be noted, even in a crowd this size.

'If you've got all the information you need for the event, I can call my driver and have him take you home. Or...there is another alternative.'

Her gaze flashed up. 'Which is...?'

'You could tell me what's wrong with you.'

'There's nothing wrong with me.' But her cheeks had gone red, branding her a liar.

'You're starting to worry me, Karina.'

'Why?'

'Because you seem lost in the past.'

'Are you surprised?' she challenged, as her night with Dante came flooding back to her.

'You're holding out on me.' Catching hold of her shoulders, he made her gasp. 'What aren't you telling me, Karina?'

She wielded her willpower like never before. 'You're right, you should stay on for the crowning of the samba queen,' she said calmly. 'That's gives me the chance to go back to the hotel so I can start putting my thoughts down on paper.'

'You can stay with me and do that later.'

He was making it impossible for her to leave without causing a scene. There was a part of her that didn't want to leave—that wanted to make up for every moment they'd been apart. And she knew how dangerous that was. 'I need some thinking time alone. I'd like to be organised when we meet to discuss the event.'

'As I would expect,' Dante agreed. 'There will be plenty of time for you to do that on my ranch.'

Her mouth dried at the thought of going to Dante's ranch. 'I need to work while my ideas are fresh,' she argued. 'You want carnival as your theme, and I'll give you carnival, but I must make my notes before all the detail of today escapes me.'

'You have all the answers, don't you?' Dante stared down at her. 'Except for the one answer I want.'

She ignored that, but not before she saw the flash of anger in his eyes. Dante liked to control everything. When she started work on his ranch she would have to make sure that Dante and his people didn't take over. This was her contract, her reputation at stake. He played on a team. Dante should be able to work with her. But would he work on her team? Her best guess was no. She maintained a diplomatic silence as they walked on side by side to the crowning.

The piazza where the celebration was to take place

was packed. Towering walls kept in the sound and the heat, creating a dizzying counterpoint to her jangling thoughts. She had always known when she had agreed to take on this project that her biggest challenge would be Dante. They were both strong characters with set ideas of their own, but he would have to learn to compromise, just as she would have to learn to keep her thoughts confined to the job.

'I'll take you back,' Dante insisted, when he saw her glance at a taxi rank.

'I can walk.'

'I won't let you. Do you think I'm going to abandon you in the middle of the city?'

She almost laughed. Feeling abandoned by Dante was hardly a new sensation for her.

The crowd was thickening as people gathered to watch the ceremony, but Dante guided her safely through with his hand in a safe place in the small of her back. It was incredible that such a light touch could have such a profound effect on her body. Why could she remember his touch so clearly? Why did those hands directing her pleasure have to spring to mind now?

Dante seemed totally at ease. He bought them both a bottle of water and a pair of flip-flops for her from a market stall so she could take off her high-heeled shoes. She groaned with pleasure as she replaced them with the simple footwear.

'Please, stop,' she begged, when he added a shawl that was billowing above them like a sail. 'You don't have to do this.'

'But I want to,' he argued, as he draped the soft jade-green fabric around her shoulders. When he drew it tighter over *that* part of her body and she flinched, he gave her a questioning stare.

'I'll need this,' she said, gazing about to distract him. 'The wind is cool at night.'

Dante stared at her for a moment, and then relaxed. 'It just reminded me of that dress you wore on your eighteenth birthday.'

Why wouldn't he remember? He had enjoyed sliding it off her.

'Your party was themed. Arabian Nights, wasn't it?'

'That's right. And as for that dress,' she added with relief, glad that he'd turned from suspicion to thinking back, 'I could hardly expect my guests to turn up in costume while I wore a suit.'

He huffed a laugh as he scanned her office outfit. 'I doubt you had one in your wardrobe. You didn't dress like an undertaker back then.'

She stroked the shawl as she remembered the soft folds of chiffon of her birthday dress beneath her hands. The outfit she had chosen to wear at her party had been floating and insubstantial...and very easy to remove.

Time to change the theme of their conversation to a safer track. 'I love the shawl. Thank you.' An involuntary quiver crossed her shoulders as his hands brushed the back of her neck. He was only lifting the shawl a little higher to protect her against the wind, but it was close enough to the danger area to make tremors of an unpleasant kind run through her. And then, thankfully, a group of people recognised him and crowded around, letting her off the hook.

'You're a complex man,' she said, when he'd signed the last autograph.

He frowned. 'I'm complex because I talk to people?'

'You're so generous with your time, and that's not the image you give out with the team.'

'Ah, the team.' His dark eyes turned black with amusement. 'The brooding and unapproachable barbarians.' He laughed. 'Do you think we would attract the same crowds if our publicist worked the image of clean-shaven, pipe-and-slippers men?'

Against her better judgement, he made her laugh. 'There's no danger of that.'

Their gazes lingered a little longer on each other's faces than perhaps they should have done, and then Dante turned serious. 'These people are my audience, Karina. Of course I respect them. I'll always make time for them. Without them I'm nothing.'

'I think you're more than you know,' she murmured to herself.

She wondered again about the years they'd been apart and Dante's meteoric rise to fame and fortune after a childhood that had been less than perfect. His father had squandered the family fortune, by all accounts, and Dante had been proud but poor. Proud, but poor and determined, she amended. There had never been anyone like him, the rumour mill said. Dante was a natural horseman, and with his looks he had soon been inundated with requests from sponsors to become the face of first this big brand and then the next. She doubted he'd had to buy a car or a watch for years, and apart from those smaller perks the money that went with the huge deals had made him an extremely wealthy man. If Dante's father could see him now...

Baracca senior had been a cold, self-serving man who could always be depended upon for one thing, and that was to be dismissive and scathing about his son. He had never been interested in what the world had thought of Dante's emerging talent because all he'd cared about had been recounting the times when he had done so much more.

'Wool-gathering again?' Dante suggested, staring keenly at her.

'I was thinking about your father.'

His expression instantly closed off, but then, to her surprise, he admitted, 'My father was an unhappy man, who was always locked in the past.'

Always trying to belittle him, she thought as Dante fell silent. She couldn't bring herself to feel charitable towards a man who had been so relentlessly critical of his own son.

CHAPTER FIVE

'Is there something wrong?' Dante asked her, when they were sitting in the car.

'I was just thinking about the logistics of accommodating thousands of people on your ranch.'

'No need to worry,' he said, cutting off her thoughts. 'My ranch is big enough to accommodate however many people want to come—and I have the funds to support them and give them the time of their lives.'

She knew a lot of wealthy people, but Dante's wealth nowadays was on a different scale. Were even those even huge contracts from sponsors enough to supply an apparently bottomless pit of money?

'So now I've reassured you, how about you open up to me?' he pressed. 'We haven't had chance to talk for years. I'd like to know what makes you tick these days, Karina.'

Her heart clenched tight. 'My work,' she said.

'There has to be more to you than that.'

'Does there?' She shrugged. 'I work—I sleep—I eat. That's it.'

He frowned. 'We used to be friends. You used to trust me.'

She bristled. She couldn't help herself. She was remembering that night. 'That was a long time ago, Dante.' She turned her head to stare out of the window.

'Butt out?' he suggested wryly.

'Something like that,' she agreed. She had buried the heartache deep where it was safe from anyone's scrutiny. At the time Dante was talking about she had thought she knew it all.

And she couldn't have been more mistaken.

They spent the rest of the journey in silence. When they arrived back at the hotel and Dante stepped out of the vehicle he was immediately surrounded by admirers. And why not, when his face was on every billboard in Rio? He had wealth beyond imagining, plus he was a notorious player in the game of life as well as on the polo field. Every woman with breath in her body wanted him.

With one notable exception, Karina told herself firmly as she got out of the car.

She stood back until Dante was on his own again, when she thanked him formally for a lovely day and for coming up with the perfect theme for the event.

'I hope today has proved productive.' He stared deep into her eyes until she had to look away. 'Are you sure you know what I want now?'

Was he still talking about the cup?

'I'm sure,' she said tightly.

'After you,' he said politely, as he waved the doorman away so he could open the door for her himself.

Following his gaze once they were inside the lobby, she stopped dead and refused to move another inch. 'Oh, no—I can't. I'm sorry.'

'You can't? Not even for an honoured client?' Smiling faintly, he lifted a brow. 'You're far too busy?' he suggested dryly.

For dancing with Dante? Yes. She should have remembered that every year after the parade her brother kept the party going by hiring one of the best samba bands in the city to entertain his guests. 'I really don't have time for dancing,' she excused herself, pinning an expression of regret to her face.

'Why not?' he asked. 'One dance with me can't hurt you, surely?'

One dance with Dante could do more damage than he knew.

'We've had a lovely day, a useful day, but now I've got so much to do.'

Her breath seemed to have taken on a life of its own as she stared at the dancers, closely packed...couples entwined...hands reaching, seeking, touching, stroking. Her chest was tight with panic and her breath was short at the thought of being pressed up hard against Dante. That was one risk she couldn't afford to take.

But Dante was determined. Taking her hand in a firm grip, he steered her onto the dance floor.

Her heart was going crazy as all the potential consequences of a simple dance swept over her. The last time she had danced with Dante had been at her eighteenth birthday party and that had led to catastrophic consequences. A harmless dance, her friends had called it, while she had laughed. She hadn't a care in the world at that time, and hadn't needed much persuasion to get up and drag Dante onto the dance floor.

She'd been up for anything then. And had fallen down a slippery slope faster than she would have ever believed possible. She stiffened now as he drew her close, and then relaxed a little because his hands were in a safe place. So long as he kept them there... She let out a tense breath when he showed no sign of moving them. He towered over her, and there was a faintly mocking and, oh, so confident expression on his face, and however hard she tried to resist him his familiar scent and strong, hard body worked its magic on her and she was lost. Dante was a rock against which her soft frame yielded all too easily.

'The perfect end to the perfect day,' he murmured in a whisper that brushed her ear. 'Now I just need you to relax.'

That was never going to happen. She came to her senses just in time, but turning to give him some smart retort she found herself staring into those mocking black eyes, and their faces were close, so close their lips were almost touching...

And then he brushed her lips with his.

Jerking her head back, she broke contact.

'For goodness' sake, Karina, what's a kiss between friends?'

Friends?

'I don't want Luc to see us,' she told him frostily.

'Luc? You care what your brother thinks?' Dante's black eyes blazed with disbelief.

'I don't think it would be very professional for him to see me kissing a client in the lobby of his hotel. It would be hard to pass that off as a business discussion, don't you think?'

Dante's massive shoulders eased in an accepting shrug, but suspicion had returned to his eyes. As well it might. There had been something so natural about their two bodies coming together. The way they moved as one would make anyone suspicious. Her body responded to Dante whether she wanted it to or not, making a dance with him more like a prelude to sex than a series of technical moves to music.

'You dance well, Karina,' he said, when the band fell silent. 'I should have remembered just how well.' She looked away from those mocking eyes. 'No, you don't,' he said, tightening his hold on her when she tried to pull away.

'I'm sure if I leave you, you won't be short of partners.'

'There's only one partner I want, and that's you.'

Dante's expression had hardened, making that a command.

'This has to stop,' she cautioned softly.

'Or we can't work together?' he suggested, with an edge of warning in his voice.

'Is that a threat?'

His answer was to dip his head and rasp his stubble against her neck, making her shudder out a gasp of indignation.

'You're shameless!'

'I'm curious,' he argued. 'Curious about you, Karina, and why you're so tense.'

She couldn't retaliate as they had attracted quite a crowd. When the national hero danced with the hotel owner's sister it was hot news and cameras on phones were flashing. There was no escape for her. She had to see this through. This was carnival season when people expected excitement and passion and, yes, hot news.

A small cry escaped her throat when Dante rubbed against her. He *was* shameless. This wasn't a quiet, safe man. He never had been. Dante's expression was knowing and mocking as he led her in the dance. He could prove so easily how much she still wanted him, just allowing her to feel the hard proof of his desire. And then the band struck up a sexy samba. She should go…

'You can't pretend you don't know the steps,' Dante insisted, murmuring the words against her ear. 'There are only three.'

There was too much laughter in his eyes for her to ignore his insistence that they have this one last dance, and willing his hands to stay where they were, and for her body to behave, she kept on dancing. Her body did the rest, with Dante's lightest, safest touch egging her on. He felt so good as they danced that she even began to relax. He felt so hard and sure, while she was so yielding and soft…

But not in the head, hopefully, she concluded, pulling away.

With a laugh Dante caught her back again. 'You're not so prim on the dance floor, are you, Senhorita Marcelos?'

'I'm doing this as a courtesy to a client and nothing more,' she said, living up to her prim tag.

'Of course you are,' Dante agreed dryly.

'And now I really do have to go,' she insisted, peeling herself away from him when the number ended.

He looked at her from beneath his brow. 'And our discussions?'

'Will be continued.' If there had been even a hint of business in his eyes she would have made an appointment with him there and then. But as it was… 'I'll get my secretary to call yours.'

He laughed at this. 'How about you call me?'

Not a chance. She had almost slipped from the straight and narrow and had no intention of risking it again. She was going to keep things formal between them from now on. 'Someone will call you,' she confirmed.

'It had better be you,' Dante warned.

She shivered involuntarily at the tone of his voice, and then gasped when he caught hold of her arm, but he was only delaying her so he could shrug off his jacket to put it around her shoulders.

'You don't need to do that—I've got my shawl.' She was wearing the shawl he'd bought her like a scarf, and had tossed it around her neck when they'd begun to dance.

'You can give the jacket back to me when you see me next,' Dante told her with a smile. Drawing it close around her, he enfolded her in his heat. 'Take your time with those notes. I want you up and running when we arrive at my *fazenda*.'

His ranch. His kingdom. His power to wield and enforce...

'You're shivering again, Karina.'

Stop fretting, or you'll make him more suspicious that ever. You can do this, she added to that instruction as she lifted her chin to stare Dante in the eyes. Deciding that making light of it was her best defence, she curved a smile. 'You've already given me your jacket. Shall I take your shirt next?'

She didn't stay to watch as Dante teased her with a wicked grin as his fingers toyed with the buttons on the front of his shirt.

She remembered those hands... She remembered those fingers...

She cursed silently, remembering what lay beneath that shirt.

It was time to forget all that and concentrate on business.

Turning on her heel, she walked away, and was more

than relieved when she reached the bank of elevators and one opened for her right on cue. Once inside she hit the button for her floor with a sigh of relief.

Dante was frustrated and pacing his bedroom with Karina on his mind. What a day it had been. Seeing her again *was* a thunderbolt. He could never have anticipated the way she made him feel. He had thought the attraction between them would have faded by now, but instead it had grown.

Yet she had catapulted away from the most innocent of kisses.

Why?

Admittedly, the kiss hadn't been all that innocent—it had been a trial, a test, an exploratory mission with motive behind it. She was hot. He was hungry. A kiss had seemed inevitable to him. He should have remembered that women harboured memories like sacred vows, while he, like most men, responded to the moment.

That insight couldn't help him now. Other woman shrank into insignificance by comparison with Karina. And she was a woman now, not a teenage siren who didn't know her own mind. She was a very beautiful woman and he wanted her. Her feelings towards him were tantalisingly ambiguous. There was the same heat between them, but there was a new reserve in her manner that he couldn't see his way past.

That wouldn't stop him trying, he accepted with a wry grin as he stopped to stretch in an attempt to ease his cramped muscles. The inactivity of city life was killing him. He longed for the freedom of the pampas. He was keen to get Karina to the ranch to see if she would relax in the setting where they'd both grown up. Luc said she hadn't visited the pampas for years, preferring life in the city. He wondered if that was true, or if she was hiding in a crowd. If that was the case, what was she running away from?

And why was he taking time out to ponder questions like that when he should be concentrating on the job she had been hired to do?

He turned as his laptop chirped and smiled thoughtfully when he saw the name at the top of the email. So she was up too. He hesitated before opening it. Karina's initial suggestions had been lacklustre. They'd been adequate, but no more than that. He hoped the trip he'd taken her on had infected her with the magic of carnival. People changed as they grew up, but he needed the old Karina's fairy dust for his event. Her flawless reputation in the events industry wasn't enough.

He had agreed to her handling the project because the Karina he'd known and grown up with could bring more than meticulous planning and attention to detail, she could bring flair and originality, but so far he'd seen little sign of that. He could only hope that fairy dust hadn't vanished in a gale of righteous living and rigid structure.

Making the decision to leave her email until a pint of coffee had fired up his brain cells, he headed for the shower. As he stepped beneath the icy water it seemed to him that in trying to protect her he had he hurt her more than he had intended. He had certainly ruined their friendship.

Karina had had the worst night's sleep ever. If she was honest, she hadn't slept at all. But she'd made good use of the hours up to dawn, spending most of them at her desk, working on an outline plan for the event. Hitting 'send', she'd sent her preliminary thoughts through to Dante. There was no point going into too much detail, because everything would need tweaking and adapting, depending on what she found at his ranch.

Her stomach plummeted at the thought. There was no getting out of it. She had to go to his ranch. Evaluating the existing facilities at the site of any new project was her first rule.

Taking herself off to shower and dress, she put on her business face along with her suit. She would meet Dante at Luc's office. Neutral territory was best. Checking her appearance one last time, she straightened her jacket and smoothed her hair. Dante was paying for her business expertise, nothing more.

How would she explain the black circles beneath her eyes?

She didn't need to explain them. Foraging in her tote, she found the concealer pen in her make-up pouch and carefully painted on some wide-awake crescents. It had shaken her, seeing him again, no question.

Shaken her? It had rocked her foundations to the core, but today would be different because today she knew what to expect and today would be all about business.

'Who put those worry lines on your face?' her brother demanded helpfully the moment she entered his office.

'I'm working. I'm preoccupied. That's *all*,' she insisted when Luc shot her a sceptical look. Flashing him an impatient glance, she began to pace his office.

'Let me guess,' he said. 'The frown has something to do with Dante?'

She turned her head and gave him her dead stare. 'Really.'

'Just don't tell me yesterday didn't go well. I heard rumours you went to carnival. Big mistake, Karina. This is business. Carnival is the wrong place to do business.'

'Says you, who spends a fortune on carnival and takes clients there. You even have a special stand erected for hotel guests, not to mention the samba band in the hotel lobby—'

'That's different,' Luc insisted.

'How is it different?'

'*I'm* different,' her brother informed her with a shrug.

'How are you different? Oh, I remember. You pee standing up.'

'Karina—'

'We had a good day, as it happens,' she said, deflecting his mocking look.

'I'm pleased to hear it. I always knew you could handle Dante.'

'I can handle him,' she confirmed. 'Shall we get started?' She glanced at her watch. 'He's late.'

'Don't you think you should wait for your client?'

'We don't know how long he's going to be.' She shrugged. 'For all we know, Dante's got something more important to do.'

Luc looked at her shrewdly. 'He has got under your skin.'

'Can we make a start, please?'

'Whatever you say.' Luc grinned with the anticipation of fun as he sat down at his desk.

'Apologies for my late arrival.'

She nearly jumped out of her skin when the door flew open. Dante's blazing stare found hers immediately.

'You're not late. We're early,' Luc pacified, smiling as he stood.

She watched the two men punch fists and hug. She

felt like an outsider when once she had been an honorary member of their gang.

That had been years ago.

She turned back to business—and tensed when Dante pulled his chair up close to hers. 'Those notes you emailed over…in the middle of the night?' His amused eyes scanned her face. 'I've taken a look at them. You get some good ideas at three o'clock in the morning. I hope I wasn't keeping you awake?'

'You weren't,' she said coolly, conscious that every part of her body was responding eagerly in spite of the fact that that was the last thing she needed. It was interesting to know Dante had been awake too, she conceded as he pushed his response notes in front of her.

'We made a good choice in your sister,' he said to Luc.

'I agree. I think Karina will do a very good job for us.'

'Excuse me—I'm sure I've mentioned this before, but I'm still here.'

'Of course you are,' Dante said warmly. 'My apologies, Senhorita Marcelos. Why don't you add to your notes a suggestion for classes so that gaucho polo players can learn better manners?'

'Good idea,' she murmured, as she studied his comments.

'I've written some notes on the back of that,' he said, leaning towards her to turn over the document she was studying.

Like an idiot, she bent her head to read, 'Dinner Cellini's. Eight o'clock.'

'Seriously?' She glanced up. 'I don't think we need to consider this, do you?'

'On the contrary *senhorita*,' Dante argued with a perfectly straight face. 'I think I've raised a very important point that should be considered right now.'

A point she was forced to award to Dante. 'Your notes are certainly comprehensive,' she agreed with a rise of her brow.

'Exactly as I intended. And your answer?'

'I'll give it some thought.' She smiled to reassure her brother, who was watching this exchange closely. She hoped Luc was oblivious to the undercurrents, though she doubted it when he asked to take a look at the page she was clutching to her chest.

'Maybe I can help clear up Dante's meaning so you can decide what to do?' he offered.

'That won't be necessary. It's perfectly clear to me.' Moving the papers out of her brother's reach, she stowed them away safely in her briefcase.

'Then can you please stop frowning so we can get on with the meeting?' Luc suggested. 'I can't tell if this is going well or not.'

And long may that last!

'Karina and I are going to work together just fine,' Dante assured Luc.

'If you say so.'

Luc looked less than convinced. And he'd better not be smiling, she thought as her brother covered his mouth with his hand. If bringing her together with Dante was his idea of a joke—

'How soon will you be going out to the *fazenda*?' Luc asked, directing his question to Dante.

It would have to be soon, Karina thought, frowning as she weighed up the hectic schedule ahead of her. There were several big projects pending—not as prestigious as this one but, then, what was? And whatever the job, she prided herself on giving it her best. But the clock was ticking.

'Tomorrow morning?' Dante suggested, turning to her to seek her approval. 'I'll have my driver pick you up.'

So soon? Her heart lurched at the thought. But that was exactly what she needed to happen, she reminded herself—not that that made the thought of going with Dante tomorrow sit any easier in her mind.

'Unless that's too soon for you, Karina?' Luc probed, seeing her frown.

'No. The sooner I can get started, the better it is for me. I have other commitments not too far down the line.'

'None that are going to interfere with this project, I trust?' Dante asked with a raised brow.

'Of course not.' Her heartbeat spiked as he continued to stare at her.

'You can't put a deputy in your place for an event like this, Karina,' he made clear.

'I know that. And it won't happen,' she assured him.

They stared at each other for a few moments longer until Luc shifted in his seat.

'I'm sorry to break this up, but I've got somewhere else to be,' her brother informed them. 'Copy me in on your reports, Karina, but wait until you've assessed the facilities at Dante's ranch before you finalise anything.'

'Of course.'

'I'll leave you two to it, then.' Luc came around the desk to shake Dante by the hand. 'I know you'll take good care of my sister.'

Karina clenched her jaw. She was as close to her brother as it was possible for siblings to be, but where Dante Baracca was concerned Luc didn't have a clue.

For the sake of maintaining a good client relationship, she called Dante to formally refuse his invitation to supper. She decided it would be better to slip it casually into the conversation with the excuse that she had to pack for the trip tomorrow. The main thrust of the call would be to ask what time she should be ready for his driver to pick her up.

'Senhor Baracca isn't taking calls, Senhorita Marcelos,' the receptionist told her, when she rang Dante at the office.

Whose bed was he in now?

Stop being ridiculous! she told herself firmly, adjusting her grip on the phone, noting that her fingers had turned white with the pressure she was applying.

'If he's not in the office, may I leave a message, please?'

'Of course. Oh—wait a minute. My apologies for not seeing this right away, *senhorita*. Senhor Baracca has left a handwritten note on my desk. He is having supper at Cellini's tonight, and expects to see you there. If you can't make it, I can try and get a message to him?'

'That won't be necessary, but thank you. I was just calling to confirm our arrangements.' She cut the line. Why shouldn't she meet up with him? Did she want Dante to think she was too affected by him to meet him out of the office? Theirs had to be a relationship of equals if she was going to work alongside him to make the polo cup the best it could be.

Dante had invited Karina to supper because he had to be sure she shared his vision for the event. He'd read her notes and was still worried she was playing it safe.

In life and in business, he mused as he drove to the restaurant, wondering why that should be so. Tonight was an opportunity for her to taste the energy and pas-

sion that brought people together and gave them the will
to create carnival. He was certain the Karina he'd once
known was still in there somewhere, and it was up to
him to strip her barriers away. He smiled at the thought.
Then he frowned. Up to now she had done everything
he'd asked, when at one time she would have challenged
every word he said. But without conflict there was no
story, and he didn't want the event he was hosting to be
a bland affair. He wanted it to be remembered for all the
right reasons, for Karina's magic, the magic he was sure
she could still bring.

The doorman took her coat and then the maître d' es-
corted her into the main body of the upscale restaurant—
where she stopped dead. Dante was certainly hosting a
supper, but it wasn't the intimate get-together she'd anticipated. Far from it. It seemed that every member of the
samba group who'd appeared at the hotel was seated at
his table, along with their mothers…and grandmothers—
and probably their aunts and cousins too, by the look of
things. And they were all dressed in their finest clothes.
She fingered the collar of her tailored office suit self-
consciously. Champagne was flowing, while the chef's
finest dishes were being carried aloft.

He'd seen her.

Dante threw a sharp glance her way. Then his face
mellowed into a look of confident amusement. She'd been
set up. He'd known what she'd think when she saw that
note. He'd put out the bait and had let her imagination to
do the rest. The look on her face must have pleased him.
It would have told him more about how she felt about
him than anything else could.

She'd make the best of it, she determined as she wove

her way through the tables. She wanted her life back, and hiding in the shadows behind her business was no way to do that.

'Karina.' Dante stood when she reached the table. 'What a pleasure,' he added. 'I'm so glad you could join us. I wasn't sure you would come.'

'I wouldn't miss this for the world,' she said, smiling at everyone.

Turning his back briefly on his guests, Dante raised an amused brow. 'I'm really pleased you're here.'

'You've already said that.'

'But I want you to know I mean it.'

As Dante stared into her eyes, her heart thundered a warning. Instead of being here and feeling the old magic washing over her, she would have been safer staying at home and banging her head against the wall in the hope of knocking some sense into it.

She had recognised some of the people around the table, and they were quick to bring her into their midst. An older lady pulled out a chair for her between herself and Dante. 'It wouldn't be complete without you here, Karina,' she said, a comment that caused Dante to swing around and stare at her with a frown.

'Thank you.' She dipped her head to hide her burning cheeks as Dante continued to scan her face with interest. What she did in her private time was none of his business.

'What did she mean?' he asked her with a frown the moment he got a chance.

'I'm an asset to any gathering?' she suggested dryly.

'That won't cut it,' he assured her, sitting back so he didn't exclude their guests.

Tough. She'd told him all she was going to.

Dante had arranged cabs to take everyone home. Before the girls and their relatives left, Karina offered the use of the hotel spa free. The older women protested that this was too much, but she insisted, and all the girls begged their relatives to relent.

'It's the least I can do,' she said. 'You all work so hard to bring pleasure to visitors from around the world.'

'And increase the business at your hotel,' Dante murmured dryly, so that only she could hear.

Ignoring him, she added, 'Just give my name at the desk and I'll make sure that you're expected.' As Dante helped her on with her jacket, she told him, 'I can see you now for half an hour to discuss flight details and any other business you might have.'

'How very good of you.' His mouth slanted in a mocking smile as he shook his head in disagreement. 'We'll talk at the ranch. I'll have my man collect you at seven prompt tomorrow morning. Don't be late.'

If looks could kill, she had just murdered the most popular man in Brazil.

CHAPTER SIX

A SECOND NIGHT without sleep was not the best of starts for a research trip. Lack of sleep made her cranky, made her vulnerable, made her brain tick slowly, and she needed her wits about her more than ever this morning. On top of sleep deprivation, being with Dante again last night had rattled her. Instead of checking that she'd got everything she needed for the trip, she was pacing up and down, waiting for dawn, fretting whether it was actually going to be possible to work alongside Dante without telling him everything.

Could she get away without telling him all of the truth? He was already suspicious about what had happened while they'd been apart, but he had no proof and no way of getting any. She wasn't such a coward that she couldn't bring herself to tell him, but was there any point in opening Pandora's box when the past couldn't be changed?

Pausing by the window, she stared down at the hotel gardens, so calm and beautiful in the moonlight. The gardens had been designed to soothe—an impossibility where she was concerned, because she was flying out of her world and into Dante's world soon, and that was a raw, unforgiving world where the secrets she was harbouring could eat her up inside.

Sitting on the edge of the bed, she put her head in her hands, thinking back to a time when they had both been wilful and unpredictable and had got away with it. They had enjoyed adventures on the pampas that made her toes curl now she thought back. The bigger the risk, the more likely they had been to take it. Then they'd grown up and life had become complicated, with innocence gone for good.

Seeing Dante again now had upended her feelings for him like a tube of sweets, shaking them out and forcing her to confront all the things she couldn't change. All the sadness she'd kept safely bottled up. She had never told anyone about losing her baby. Who could she tell? Luc? Dante? The medical team had said she was 'lucky' because she had lost her child in the relatively early stages of pregnancy. She hadn't felt lucky. She'd felt devastated. When she'd left the hospital and even the kind attention of the medical professionals had been taken away, she had felt alone, grief-stricken, with no consolation to be found anywhere. It had been a very long and slow road back to recovery, and she wasn't even sure she'd reached her destination yet.

Maybe she never would. Closing her arms over her head as if that could block out the nightmare, she tensed as the scene played out in her head. She had asked the lady operating the scanner if her baby was dead, as if by some miracle the little light she had cherished for so short a time could still find a way to shine. There was no reason for it, the doctor had told her. Nature could be cruel. And once was enough to get pregnant, he had added disapprovingly when she had least needed to hear that.

Once with Dante.

She'd been too young, too inexperienced to handle something like that on her own, the same medical team had advised. But she'd had to handle it. Her mother was dead. She couldn't say a word to her brother and risk breaking his heart. It would have destroyed the team, set him against Dante. Worse, it would have destroyed her brother's trust in her, and how could she do that after everything Luc had done for her when their parents had died? She loved her brother too much to put him through that. He would never know.

Why hadn't she told Dante?

Lifting her head, she gave a sad smile. Practising the art of making babies was Dante's specialty. Dealing with the aftermath? Not so much.

But this wasn't all on Dante. According to what she'd overheard when they'd been younger, he'd had a life as a child that no one could envy. It was no wonder that he'd cast about, trying to find love. She was no better. At age eighteen she was supposed to know it all. She had certainly thought she did, and that was the impression she'd given Dante at the party. And he'd used protection. What more was he supposed to do when she had been an all-too-willing partner?

It had been bravado in front of her friends that night. She had wanted to take the bond, the friendship she'd had with Dante and move it on to the next level—preferably before one of her girlfriends landed him. She'd taken the initiative, and she had led him to her room where hot, hungry nature had taken its course.

She should have told him she was a virgin, but she could hardly do that after putting on such an air of experience. She was lucky he had prepared her so well that all she remembered was pleasure. And it had been more than once. They had made love throughout the night. Well, she had. Dante had had sex with her. Maybe he wasn't capable of anything more…maybe his ruined childhood had numbed him to feelings.

It certainly hadn't affected his stamina. That had been inexhaustible. He had been inventive and had known how to use every surface in the room. She had never expected anything like it, and knew for a fact she would never experience anything like it again.

What a klutz. What an eighteen-year-old klutz. She should have known that every action had a consequence. She might have anticipated Dante would throw her out of his bed. What else was he going to do? Marry her? Marry a girl on the threshold of life, who'd been his friend and who had taken that friendship and mangled it?

And now she was going to leave the security of her job in the city, with a brother who cherished and cared for her, for the wilds of the pampas with a man she hardly knew these days.

What were her options? Back down and throw away the chance of a lifetime because she was too scared to face the past? Appoint someone else in her place to handle the job? Dante had ruled that out from the start. And she could never live with herself if she did that. Should she live out her life in the shadows from now on, never admitting what she wanted, which was to be judged on her own merits—merits that felt thin and few right now?

It all came back to Dante. When she had discovered she was pregnant, she'd hung on, trying to find the right time to approach him and tell him, but he'd become elusive, moving in such sophisticated company she'd rarely seen him, except from a distance at a match. When she'd lost the baby, nothing else had mattered, and she'd been too bruised to face the rigmarole of trying to convince Dante that he was the father of her child—the child she'd lost. What was the point when there was no child? And so she'd kept her secret all these years.

And then she'd embarked on her fightback, going to college abroad, where she had got her head down and learned what had been expected of her in the hotel trade, which had been to be impeccably groomed at all times, and to have the type of quiet manners that reassured people.

How would Dante react if she told him all that now?

He'd be furious and rightly so, and she couldn't risk alienating him so close to the polo cup, though with his suspicions already roused she might be forced to tell him. He could always read her. She couldn't use the argument that many youthful friendships didn't survive the changes in people, and that they'd moved away and apart, and there'd never been chance to tell him about the baby—she couldn't do it, because that tiny light still shone too brightly in her mind, and the bond between her and Dante was still so strong.

Once they were isolated on his *fazenda* could she lie to him? Or would she tell him the truth and face the consequences?

As Dante's sleek executive jet descended to a smooth landing on the narrow airstrip, Karina was both apprehensive and excited, as well as interested in what she'd find at his home. How would the world-famous barbarian live? She knew so little about him these days. Her brother didn't dabble in gossip of any kind. Bottom line. She really didn't know anything about him. He might as well be a stranger she was visiting. And she shouldn't be remotely interested. Staring out at the endless swathes of emerald green and gold pampas, she reassured herself that it wasn't necessary to understand the ins and outs of a client's private life in order to do business with them.

'We are here, *senhorita*…'

She glanced up into the smiling eyes of the cabin attendant. Gathering her belongings, she unfastened her seat belt and got ready to disembark.

She must stop thinking about Dante, she warned herself as the jet engine died to a petulant whine. Her glance had flashed instantly to the cockpit door. She would see him soon enough. They'd be working together, remember?

'*Senhorita?*'

She followed the flight attendant to the exit door. And blinked as she inhaled her first lungful of warm, herby air. Even laced with aviation fuel, it was familiar and intoxicating. She'd been away too long. But now she was home. Closing her eyes, she lifted her face to the sun. If it was possible to be changed in a moment, she was changed. But not so changed that she had forgotten why she was here. She ran through a quick mental checklist of everything she'd brought with her. She was still a professional, even if the lure of the pampas was strong in her blood. And she was still determined to handle Dante a lot better than she had at eighteen.

'*Senhorita?*'

'Sorry.' She smiled as the flight attendant indicated that she might like to exit the aircraft—preferably some time this year, Karina guessed with a rueful grin.

Reality hit as she walked down the steps. She smoothed an imaginary crease in her jeans with damp palms as

she took in the fact that this wasn't her land, this was
Dante's land. He lived his unknown life here. She wished
she'd dressed up a bit more, to add to her confidence and
to reinforce her professional image. She had chosen to
dress casually for the flight, as it wouldn't have been a
surprise to find that Dante had two wild horses waiting to transport them bareback to his ranch. She'd got
that badly wrong. There was no sign of Dante, but there
were two top-of-the-range off-road vehicles waiting on
the tarmac. The one closest to the aircraft had a young
gaucho standing by the passenger door, who nodded to
her as she hesitated.

'Welcome to Fazenda Baracca, Senhorita Marcelos.'

'Karina, please,' she replied with a smile.

'Gabe. Ranch manager.'

Gabe's handshake was brisk and firm, and he was
about a foot taller than she was, though not as tall as
Dante.

'Senhor Baracca sends his apologies, but he may not
join you today.'

From this she assumed Dante meant to keep her on
tenterhooks. Good luck with that, she thought, firming
her chin. She was here to work, not to idle her time away,
waiting for him.

'He has his usual checks to carry out,' Gabe explained,
seeing her expression change. 'He asks that you make
plans to tour the ranch tomorrow, and meanwhile he asks
that you make yourself at home and get to work on your
plans for the cup.'

Was that a rain check or a reprieve?

Thanking Gabe, she settled into the passenger seat
and he closed the door. She stared around with interest.
Dante's land radiated order and care. From the pristine

fencing around the paddocks stretching away towards
the horizon to the impeccable airstrip, where his private
jet sat like a gleaming white bird, it was obvious that
no expense had been spared. This was gaucho polo in a
diamond-studded frame. She was already excited at the
thought of organising an event here. She'd known Dante
was rich—all the polo guys were wealthy—but this was
money on a vast scale.

Inevitably, she began to brood. Where had the money
come from? Dante's parents had lived beyond their
means, as far as she could remember. Her parents' ranch
had enjoyed much better facilities, which was why Dante
and all the other young polo hopefuls had come there to
train. Dante held several valuable franchises now he was
so successful, but was that enough for a private jet, this
ranch and his glittering lifestyle?

She jolted alert, as Gabe called out through his open
window. Dante was just climbing behind the wheel of
the second off-road vehicle. His eyes were hidden behind dark glasses, but he raised a hand when he saw
her looking. Then he started the engine and drove away.
His interest in her was as fleeting as it got, as if it was
enough for him to check her transfer from jet to ranch
was going smoothly.

That suited her fine, she told herself firmly. Settling
back in her seat, she turned her mind to the project. Everything she saw and experienced from this moment on
might be crucial to the polo cup. Nothing must escape
her notice. She had to be like a sponge and soak it all up.
She had no idea what to expect. She had only visited the
Baracca ranch a couple of times as a child, and had never
been invited into the main house. She remembered it as
being dark and forbidding. Money had been tight for the

Baraccas, her mother had explained, because of the high life Dante's father made sure he enjoyed.

Gabe drove cross-country for around ten minutes before they reached some imposing gates. These marked the formal entrance to the main ranch house complex, he explained. The entrance had been pulled back considerably since the last time she had visited. Opening the window, she leaned out to stare around with interest. The barns and buildings had been developed and improved to the point where the run up to the ranch house was more like a drive through a well-ordered village set in a beautiful emerald-green frame than a potholed track flanked by the rotting buildings she remembered.

Mellow stone and burnished wood combined beneath a sultry sun to turn Dante's large ranch house a soft, shimmering bronze, while a frame of trees added shade and coolness to the entrance. She was impressed. More importantly, for the purposes of the polo cup, visitors would be impressed.

Her excitement for the project was building. There wasn't a thing out of place. The vivid floral displays in the formal grounds around the house were breathtaking. The image visitors would carry away would be that of a perfect ranch, with perfect grounds and perfect animals happily grazing. She could see the flyers and the brochures she'd have printed now, showing warm wood, sun-kissed stone and white paintwork, flanked by brilliantly coloured flowers and emerald-green paddocks stretching away into the distance, with choice groupings of well cared-for animals. This year's polo cup was shaping up to be the easiest event she'd ever been asked to promote.

She had to organise it first, Karina reminded herself as the familiar excitement rose inside her. It was tinged with a slight attack of nerves as she considered the enormity of the task ahead of her, but she put those aside for now to smile at Gabe as he drew up outside the open front door, where a beaming housekeeper was waiting to welcome them.

'I can't believe the changes here since the last time I visited.'

'That must have been some time ago,' he commented. 'Dante has renovated everything, and the main house has been added to substantially since he's been in charge.'

'Have you worked here long?'

'For the past few years—since Dante's other interests started taking up more of his time.'

His other interests?

'I've got my own spread,' Gabe explained. 'This is a temporary placement—a favour for Dante. He's done a lot to help me build up my own breeding programme and so I said I'd help him out. He assures me that he's going to settle down here one day,' Gabe added with a wry look. 'But so far no sign of that.'

So he hadn't settled down. Her heart thundered and her brain was clicking. What other interests could Dante possibly have? Surely the ranch and his polo took up all his time? A glance at Gabe's face suggested he would be no more forthcoming than Dante.

'Did you know his father?'

Gabe stared at her for a few long seconds before volunteering in a lazy drawl, 'I've heard about him.'

It wouldn't be anything complimentary, she guessed. Apart from instinctively not liking Dante's father, she remembered her mother saying Dante had *saved* his mother from his bullying father. She'd been too young to remember the detail. It still sent a shiver down her spine. His mother's suffering had been bad enough, and the thought of the things Dante must have seen and endured as a child made her feel sad for him.

'I didn't really know Senhor Baracca senior that well myself. Strange really when you consider that Dante, my brother and I spent endless days on this ranch as kids. It was an amazing setting for any child. Though I don't suppose there are any children on the ranch now?' she queried curiously.

Gabe exploded with laughter. 'No children?' he echoed. 'I hope you're not allergic to the little brutes, because you're going to find hordes of them here.'

'Hordes?' she questioned, but Gabe wasn't giving anything away.

'What about you, Karina?' he pressed. 'Family?'

'No.' Her voice sounded strained, but she found a smile to reassure Gabe.

'You must love your job to make it everything,' he said, staring at her keenly.

'Yes, I do.' It helped her to live with the memories by taking up so much of her time, and she was looking forward to escaping the safety net Luc had always provided for her. She wanted to taste life, to try and learn to live with the past, and where better to do that than here on the pampas she had almost forgotten she loved so much?

'Hey, Dante!'

Her heart leapt into her mouth as she swung around to follow Gabe's greeting. She was just in time to see Dante vault a fence as he went to check on some horses in the paddock.

His virility shocked her. How could she have forgotten?

She hadn't forgotten, but in this setting it seemed more

pronounced than ever. Dante was brutally masculine, so strong and hard-muscled—and yet so gentle and affectionate towards the horse, she noticed. Animals loved him, and she loved watching his interaction with them. There was nothing left of the polished businessman here, or even the startlingly good-looking playboy featured in so many magazines. Dante was a gaucho through and through, and here on his *fazenda* he was at home, back in control of his land.

She tensed as he raised a hand to acknowledge Gabe, noticing how Dante's black stare remained fixed on her.

CHAPTER SEVEN

KARINA WAS REALLY HERE. Forget the checks he usually made on his return to the ranch. Gabe could handle them. Dante felt alive—more alive than ever before. His senses were on full alert, with every instinct he possessed honed to the sharpest point. Having Karina on his ranch and under his roof was like warm honey singing through his veins. They'd been apart too long. And here there could only be truth between them. The pampas was too vast, too beautiful, too unforgiving to allow for human short-comings. It revealed and exposed. It was harsh and true. It brought out the best in people…and the worst.

Seeing Karina here took him back to the past, a place he usually avoided. It was never easy to remember the way his father had treated his mother, not even trou-bling to hide his countless infidelities. His father had seen these as proof of his virility, rather than a tragedy that had broken his mother's heart. He glanced at the ranch house his mother had called home, and which he had renovated in her memory, knowing the housekeeper would be settling Karina in, and she would be meet-ing up with the happy chaos that characterised his life-style. He smiled to himself as he wondered what she'd make of it.

* * *

The housekeeper welcomed Karina into a vaulted hall-way where the noise levels were off the scale. Gabe was right. There were hordes of children. Which was the last thing she had expected of Dante.

'*Descuplas!* My apologies!' the housekeeper, who had introduced herself as Maria, exclaimed with an indulgent laugh as she took hold of Karina's arm to steer her out of the way of a makeshift raft on wheels manned by several youngsters. 'Today is a very special day. The master is home and everyone is excited.'

Dante, the master of all he surveyed? Karina smiled, admitting to herself that she felt completely at home here in the chaos. Riding tack and footballs, along with dis-carded toys and a number of junior bicycles piled up in a heap competed for space with sturdy antique furniture, polished to within an inch of its life.

'So?' She jumped at the sound of the deep male voice. 'What do you think of my home, Karina? Do you ap-prove?'

'Dante!' She spun on her heel. 'I didn't expect to see you here today.'

'Why?' He shrugged. 'This is my home.'

'Gabe said—' She bit her tongue and let it go. Dante was entitled to change his mind.

'Do you like what I've done with the house?' he prompted, giving her a look that made her stomach clench with pleasure rather than alarm.

He was talking about the mess, which she didn't care about at all. It was a happy home. She could feel that right away. And that was all that mattered.

'As it happens, I like it a lot,' she said.

'Good.'

Dante's deep, husky voice shivered through her like a hot knife through melting meringue. His wicked smile was something she hadn't seen enough of, though he was making it increasingly hard for her to confine her thoughts to business. It didn't help that he was as tall and as dark and as devastatingly handsome as he'd ever been—but not quite so menacing now that he had a group of children clinging to his legs.

Even as she took all this in, she felt her frantic city life drop away and the pampas claim her. She felt different. Even Dante looked different here, and the longing to ride free and wild with him was suddenly overwhelming.

'I'm going to the kitchen to grab some food with these urchins,' he said. 'Join me when you've settled in, and then we'll discuss my agenda.'

Dante had changed? Maybe not that much! She held back on a salute. 'I trust you'll be equally open to discussing my agenda?'

'That all depends on what your agenda is...'

He held her stare a beat too long, his mouth slanted in a challenging smile and his eyes glowing with an emotion she couldn't read. She still hadn't figured out where the children fitted into his lifestyle, and was halfway up the stairs when a female voice called out, 'Karina?'

Her stomach contracted as she turned around. The girl was very beautiful.

'Honestly, they're impossible,' the mystery girl exclaimed, shaking a play fist at the children. 'You're very brave to come here.'

Karina got over her initial reaction fast. She liked the girl on sight. 'It looks like fun to me.' She smiled down.

'I'm Nichola, but everyone calls me Nicky. Sorry!

Can't shake your hand. I'm covered in finger-paint.' Nicky brandished both hands palms up as proof.

'You're in charge of the children?'

'In charge?' Nicky's laughter pealed out as she thought about that. 'That's one way of putting it! I love them, but I'm always glad to hand them back to their parents. But what about you? Apparently, you're amazing—according to Dante,' she explained, when Karina looked surprised. 'The children from the families of those who work on the ranch treat this as their second home,' Nicky explained, 'and Dante brings more in from the city to experience life on a ranch. He says he loves the place to be used, and I'm usually around, a bit like an adoptive auntie, I suppose, which in a way I am, being Dante's sister…'

'Sister?' Karina queried, thinking back. She couldn't remember Dante having a sister.

'You were away, I expect, when I moved in, or you'd have heard all about me. I'm Dante's father's love child,' Nicky explained, with the same openness that had drawn Karina to her. 'Not that there was much love involved, from what I can understand.'

Were there any similarities between father and son? A knot snagged in Karina's stomach.

'Dante's mother brought me here to live with them when my own mother died,' Nicky explained. 'Things weren't easy for Dante's mother, but I suppose you know that—it was common knowledge. That didn't stop her taking me in. You probably remember, that was the sort of woman she was.'

'A saint,' Karina agreed, as pieces of the jigsaw that made up the life of Dante Baracca flew together at break-neck speed. 'I'm only sorry I didn't get the chance to know Dante's mother better. I only met her a few times when I was a child, but my mother used to talk about how good she was.'

Nicky shared her grimace as they thought back. 'Dante's father liked to keep her out of the way—kitchen sink or his bed were her only permitted zones, from what I can understand.'

Karina guessed they both felt the same shiver run down their spines, but Nicky soon lightened the mood with her smile. 'Sorry. I'm keeping you from settling in. Let Maria show you to your room—I have to pack anyway, as I'm leaving soon.'

'You're leaving?' Karina was disappointed, having found someone she believed could be a friend.

'Yes.' Nicky heaved a mock sigh. 'Dante will have to fend for himself, though my best guess is that his adoring staff will do the fending for him, leaving Dante free to bring in more waifs and strays.'

'Waifs and strays?' Karina was beginning to feel like a parrot, but this was so much information in the space of a couple of minutes she couldn't get things straight in her head.

'Dante has a plan for the future,' Nicky revealed enigmatically.

There was only one certainty, Karina concluded when Nicky headed off across the hall. Every preconceived notion she'd had about Dante Baracca had been turned upside down.

'I'd make the most of having the day to yourself today if I were you,' Nicky shouted back to her. 'Knowing Dante, he'll be knocking on your door at cockcrow in the morning. Just remember the fun starts tomorrow, so make the most of the peace and quiet today.'

Karina's head was spinning, but it was hard not to be

optimistic when Maria ushered her into the most beautiful guest room. Light and bright, it was beautifully decorated in shades of ice blue and coral. If it hadn't been for Dante and the history they shared, she would have been more thrilled than ever to be back on the pampas she loved, especially when Maria threw back the drapes to reveal a wide, deep balcony overlooking fields full of foals and their mothers. What more could she possibly want than this?

Answers?

Her life was what she'd made it, though it was impossible not to think about Dante and try to piece together the nuggets of information Nicky had shared. Did Dante take after his cold, self-serving father or after his mother, a woman who had cared enough to bring the orphaned child of her husband's mistress into her home?

That was a question for another day, Karina concluded as Maria suggested that Nicky's idea was a good one, and that tonight Karina might like to take supper in her room later.

'I would. Thank you.' She'd spend the rest of the day working on her laptop, then a hot, foamy bath beckoned, before food and bed. Something told her she would need her sleep, and that tomorrow would be soon enough to start piecing together the puzzle that was Dante Baracca.

She had barely finished her shower the next morning when she heard the clatter of hooves outside her open window. Grabbing a couple of towels, she covered herself and padded barefoot to the window. And shot back, seeing Dante on horseback. Her heart was racing, arguing with all the sensible plans she had made to be detached where he was concerned, and above all sensible. It didn't matter that they had both grown up and moved on in ten years, or that Dante was now a client whose sole intention was to show her the facilities on his ranch. It was enough that he was out there, looking as sexy as sin, for her heart to pound ten to the dozen.

'Hey, Karina!'

Firming her jaw, she stared out as if she saw a man who looked as rugged and sexy as Dante every day of the week. The impatient look he was giving her suggested that by sheer willpower alone he believed he could draw her down from the window and onto the saddle of the horse at his side. Let him stare. She'd just got out of the shower. Dante might have the turnaround capabilities of a holiday jet, but that didn't mean she had to rush about. She would behave calmly and act professionally, as she always did.

'Good morning. Can I help you?' she asked politely.

'I want you down here now.'

She flashed five fingers, indicating more time was required.

'And I don't have all day to waste,' Dante growled threateningly.

His expression made her think one finger would have been enough.

Taking the full five minutes, she tied her hair back, and changed into breeches and shirt. She was neat, she was organised. She was ready.

For anything.

Which was probably just as well, as Dante had undergone the full gaucho transformation. His wild black hair was held back by a blood-red bandana and his gold earrings glinted in the sun. He was wearing well-worn, snug-fitting jeans beneath the battered leather chaps all

the gauchos wore, and a tight-fitting black top emphasised his bunched and banded muscles. Could she blank
her mind to that?

She could blank her mind, but her body had a will
of its own, and her nipples rose to salute him when she
joined Dante in the yard.

'So you're ready at last?' Looking her up and down
with a lazy smile, he handed over the reins of her horse.

She knew that look and gave him one back that said
clearly, *You're wasting your time.* She didn't sleep with
clients, however 'honoured' they might be. She never
had. She didn't sleep with anyone, come to that. How
could she? Dante might be the most tempting piece of
forbidden fruit around, but she had to think of him as
the spoiled fruit the wasp had got to first. If she did that
she'd be fine. It was that, or risk getting her heart broken all over again.

'I take it you can still remember how?'

She looked at him as she checked her horse's girth, and
that look said it all. They both knew horses could hold
air in their lungs when the strap beneath their belly was
fastened, and then they let it out again once the rider was
mounted, causing the saddle to slip dangerously. Guessing the type of ride she was about to have with Dante,
she was going to take every safety precaution necessary.
Springing into the saddle, she gave him a look. 'I think
I'll keep up.'

Closing her eyes for a moment as she sucked in a lungful of sweet, clean air, she promised herself that nothing
was going to spoil this for her. This was her first ride
on the pampas for too long, and she was going to enjoy
it to the full. She would learn everything she needed to

about his ranch, and then she'd go home to plan the event, happy, single and sane.

Dante led off at a canter, issuing information and instructions as he rode. His facilities were world-class. She had a rough idea of what a set-up like this must have cost. Her brother maintained a vast and well-equipped stud, but Dante's equestrian centre was on another level again. He had built a full-sized polo club that would have sat proudly in any country, and there was the best accommodation possible for visiting horses, riders and grooms. She already knew about the veterinary hospital and exercise pools, because Gabe had pointed them out to her, but now she discovered there was an Olympic-size swimming pool for their human guests.

'You live in some style,' she commented wryly when they finally reined in.

'Don't you approve?'

'It's not up to me to judge you.'

'But you do judge me, don't you, Karina?'

Before she could reply, Dante turned his horse and was soon lost in the distance, a silhouette against the vast blue sky. He was like a dark angel, brooding and powerful, and for now she was left in pursuit. Urging her horse forward, she caught up with him.

'Where are we going?' she asked, riding alongside him.

Turning to slant an amused look at her, he chose to ignore the question. 'You still ride well, Karina.'

'I always could keep up with you,' she commented dryly.

'But you never used to be so suspicious.'

'And neither did you,' she pointed out. 'But that was a long time ago, Dante.'

When neither of them had cause to be suspicious of each other, she thought as his black stare levelled on her face.

Relaxing in the saddle with just one hand on the reins, he shifted his weight almost imperceptibly and his big black horse took off again.

Leaning low over her horse's neck, she gave him his head. At least riding was as good as she remembered. Her anxieties and suspicions remained, as did the ghosts from the past, but gradually she was relaxing in a way she had never found possible in the city. Maybe the pampas was where she had to be in order to lay those ghosts.

'There you are,' he murmured, when she trotted up.

'You have a bigger horse,' she pointed out logically, finding the pride of her youth, where competing with Dante was concerned, was still one hundred per cent intact.

He shrugged. 'Change horses and I'll still ride faster than you.'

She weighed up his stallion. 'Would you care to put that to the test?'

They dismounted.

The stallion's acceleration was phenomenal. It was like sitting on a rocket...*or on Dante*. Her laughter was carried away on the breeze. She hadn't felt like this for years. She was soon well in front, with confidence thrilling through her. How could she have forgotten how good riding with Dante felt?

'What?'

She gasped with outrage when he suddenly appeared in front of her. 'How did you do that?'

There was no chance he could hear her. He was half a mile ahead. Whispering in the stallion's ear, she left the big horse in no doubt as to what he had to do. She hadn't raced like this with Dante since they had been kids riding wild on the range, and she'd have to brush up her skills, as well as the tricks they used to play on each other, if she was going to stand a chance of keeping up. Doggedly, she turned his big stallion in Dante's direction, and when she finally caught up they exchanged horses without a word.

'There must be a lot of things you want to ask me,' he commented as they left their reins loose and allowed the horses to choose the way for a while. 'Well?' he prompted. 'Or are you concerned I might do the same to you?'

His stare on her face was level and hard, and she realised how tense she could so quickly become under his scrutiny. Having picked up the reins and shortened them as if for flight, she was gripping them as if her life depended on it. She wanted to say something, make some excuse, but words wouldn't come, and with a last cold and knowing look into her eyes Dante gathered up his reins and rode away.

CHAPTER EIGHT

KARINA WAS HOLDING out on him, and trust was essential if they were going to work together successfully. He'd replayed the night they'd slept together over and over in his head, and he was more confident than ever that he'd done the right thing. He could maybe have dressed things up a bit better, but he'd been younger then, and impulsive.

'Dante?'

Karina was looking at him with concern.

'Is something wrong?' she pressed, glancing away as if she knew very well that he expected her to be more open with him.

'Time is short, and we've got a lot of ground to cover,' he said curtly. His questions would have to wait. They had too much to do to waste time on conversation outside the event they were planning. He led the way through a group of trees planted to screen some groundwork and then reined in.

'What's this?' Karina asked, as she stared down at the ugly gash in the land.

It was the only blemish on his otherwise flawless ranch, but it was one that paid for his lifestyle and for everything that visitors to the polo cup would enjoy. 'It's an emerald mine.'

'Are you serious?' Karina's shocked gaze flashed to his.
'Perfectly.'

She frowned and he could almost see her thinking that this answered a lot of her questions about the source of his immense wealth. 'Is it yours?'

'I have a major stake in it,' he confirmed.

'At least it explains your Midas touch.' She relaxed as she smiled—with relief, he guessed.

'So now you know my secret.'

'One of them.' She stared at him steadily. 'Nicky said you had plans for the future. Plans involving the youngsters who come to the ranch?'

He stonewalled her question with a question of his own. 'No secrets of your own to share?'

'No,' she said flatly, clearly irritated that he wouldn't share the smallest detail with her. 'My life would bore you, and even if that weren't the case, I don't see how it's relevant to our business discussions.'

'One ride across the pampas is hardly going to restore the friendship of our youth.'

'I hope you can trust me in business?'

He raised a brow. 'So do I.'

'So,' she said, clearly keen to change the subject, 'can we have tours here on the days of the tournament, or would security be an issue for you?'

'We can have tours,' he confirmed.

'Good,' she said stiffly. 'I'll add them to my list.'

'Shall we move on?' he suggested.

She was holding out on him. Each time he looked at Karina her eyes darkened and her lips plumped up, as every female hormone she possessed danced with his machismo. She'd pulled back in Rio rather than risk kissing him, and she was still reluctant to share the smallest personal detail with him. *Why?*

'You look thunderous,' she commented, as they cantered along side by side. 'Has some detail of my planning annoyed you? If you'd rather leave the tour to the emerald mine out...'

A muscle flexed in his jaw as he stared straight ahead. She'd seen his home. She was living under the same roof as him, *pelo amor de Deus!* And now she'd seen the emerald mine. He was running out of surprises to try and jolt Karina into sharing whatever it was that was eating away at her. What was so bad she couldn't tell him?

'Why don't you tell me more about the mine, Dante?' she said in an attempt to restore normality. It made his hackles rise even more. She'd pick any topic to stop him questioning her, but for the sake of their *working relationship* he'd go along with it—for now.

'Mining isn't my specialty, though there have always been old workings here,' he explained. 'The old-timers talked constantly about the green ice they used to find here—that's what they call emeralds—so I decided to investigate. I sold the exploration rights and brought in experts. I used the same consortium that revived the Skavanga diamond mine in northern Europe. The deal was that I got to keep a share in whatever they found. It turned out to be one of the richest seams of emeralds in the world.'

She laughed—with relief at the relaxation in the tension between them, or with genuine pleasure at this discovery of unsuspected riches, he couldn't tell.

'I'm not really surprised now I've got over the shock of you owning an emerald mine,' she confessed, smiling at him. 'I can't imagine you doing anything on a small scale.'

'Not if I can help it,' he agreed, tight-lipped. Urging his horse forward, he put some much-needed thinking space between them.

She allowed her horse to pick its own way down the slope as she considered the tension in Dante. His back was like an unbreachable wall. Suspicion was riding him, and so far she'd told him very little, but she wouldn't be rushed into anything. She'd choose her time.

When?

Soon.

To break the tension between them, she decided on a change of subject when she caught up with him. 'I met your half-sister, Nicky. She's lovely.'

'She's great,' Dante agreed tersely.

'Who takes care of the children when she's not here on the ranch?'

'Why? Are you volunteering, Karina?'

'No.' She huffed a wry laugh. 'I've got my own job to do.'

'Relieved?' Dante suggested.

She shrugged. 'No, but those kids are quite something.' She paused, hoping Dante would tell her more, but he wasn't so easy to unravel.

'The staff will take over.' He shrugged.

Dante took off again at speed, preventing her asking him any more questions. Hooves were soon thundering beneath them, making any form of conversation impossible, but she guessed Dante would want more answers when they got back to the ranch. She slowed her horse, allowing him to ride ahead of her, just to drink him in.

There was no law against glutting herself on powerful shoulders and hard-muscled arms. She had always loved watching Dante ride. He appeared so casual and yet he was fully in control, with one hand on the reins and the other relaxed at his side. He rode smoothly and efficiently, employing minimum effort for maximum result.

Much as he'd ridden her.

Air shot from her lungs at the rogue thought entered her head. She had to shake herself round fast, and then she realised that Dante had turned his horse and was coming back for her.

'What are you waiting for?' he demanded. 'Reminiscing?'

'No. Thinking forward,' she argued firmly.

'About?'

'About the work we have to do, and the short time we have to complete it in.'

'*You* have to complete it in,' he stressed with a look. 'If you're having second thoughts about your ability to handle a project as big as this one, you'd better let me know right away.'

'I'm not having second thoughts.' She met his demanding stare head on. 'I'll get this job done in good time, and it will be something we can both be proud of.'

'It isn't enough for me that you get it done. I expect more from you than that. And as for me being proud?' He frowned. 'It's more important to me that I feel passion coming from you where this job is concerned. I want you to inspire the people who visit my ranch. That's the only way you'll make something memorable out of this.'

'It will be memorable.' She matched him with all her old fire.

'That's all I need to hear,' Dante confirmed, turning away.

She watched him ride off, marvelling that she had ever been so young and naïve as to believe they would stay together just because they'd slept together. Anything had seemed possible on that magical night. Consequences hadn't even crossed her mind. Dante had made her feel so safe.

Had he?

Wasn't it more likely that she had embroidered the facts to fit her fantasy version of a relationship with Dante? Everything about that night had been reckless— from the flimsy dress she had chosen to wear, to her dancing and then their lovemaking. An eighteenth birthday was supposed to mark the transition from childhood to adulthood, but she'd had to take everything to the edge. The validation of everything she'd been, and everything she'd hoped to be, had seemed to lie in the hands of one man—until Dante had thrown her out. Which she now understood had probably been a good thing, though it hadn't seemed so at the time.

Good, because everything since that moment had made her face up to the fact that it was up to her to make her own fate, search out her own opportunities and her own path through life. Before the party she had still believed in fairy tales, and had saved herself for Dante. She had taken what had been a childhood friendship and changed it in her mind into true love, believing she'd touched him somewhere deep.

It had been a real slap in the face to discover that she hadn't touched Dante anywhere. He had a deadline to keep, he had told her that night as he'd stared pointedly at the floor where her clothes lay scattered. He'd told her to pick them up and get out. She could still remember her shock as she'd stared at him numbly, trying to work out what she'd done wrong. 'Take a shower and get out,' he'd barked as she'd scooped up her clothes as if he couldn't wait to get rid of her. She remembered holding them against her body, feeling suddenly ashamed of her nakedness.

'Why are you frowning?' Dante demanded, jerking her out of her recollections.

If love were a fairy tale, Dante had got the frog and prince thing completely wrong!

'Are you going to dismount and let your horse drink?' he prompted.

She sprang down to the ground before he could help her out of the saddle. She didn't want to risk him touching her.

'I'd like your opinion on this living accommodation…'

She refocused rapidly to take in the block of luxury apartments in front of them, and then realised they had ridden down a pathway flanked by the most beautiful gardens.

'This is spectacular,' she gasped, as she stared around. 'It's like an oasis in the desert. It's ideal for what we need. Can we go inside and take a closer look?'

'This is where we'll house the VIPs during the cup,' he called back as he led the way.

It was hard to believe they had ever lain in bed together, or that they had known each other as intimately as any couple could. His broad, muscular back was turned against her, making him seem like a stranger.

The building was so striking, it took her mind off her troubled thoughts for a while. The block of apartments curved in a horseshoe around the banks of a glittering manmade lake. When she stepped inside she was silenced as she stared around the light-filled space.

'There's a hot spa and a small heated outdoor pool for each apartment, as well as a butler service on call,' Dante explained.

'Butlers on horseback?'

'In helicopters. It's faster.'

'Of course.' Somehow she managed to keep a straight face. She had a lot of wealthy clients who had all sorts of unimaginable luxuries they took for granted, but in all her experience she had never heard of anything to compare with this.

'Take your time to look around. I'm going to leave you to it, while I inspect the rest of the units to make sure they're all up to the standard I requested.'

He filled every inch of her world with heat and machismo, and he made her ache with wistfulness for everything they'd lost; a loss he didn't even know about. She quickly busied herself making notes, as he paused and turned to face her.

'There's just one thing you need to keep in mind,' he said. 'The Goucho Cup means everything to me. The game is my passion, and it's a passion I want to share with the world. I'm determined to prove that it isn't a game for a privileged few but an exciting spectator sport. I'm going to need your help to make that dream a reality. Are you in?'

'You know I am.' How could she not be infected by his enthusiasm, or by Dante's dark, compelling stare?

Those few moments of intensity between them left her reeling, and it was almost a relief to move on to discussing food outlets and supply chains, though there was a moment later in the day when he turned to her to demand, 'Who would have thought fate would throw us together again like this?' But then he shook his head and snapped, 'Forget it.'

That was one thing she couldn't do. Fate had always meant them to be together—just not in the way she had expected.

CHAPTER NINE

WHEN THEY RETURNED to the ranch house she made the excuse that she needed a chance to compile her notes. Dante was way too distracting, and she was glad of some space. She ate alone and went straight to bed, but she couldn't sleep.

Getting up, she worked through the night. There was a point in the cold dark hours when she wondered if frustration could actually cause a physical ache. The pain when she thought about Dante seemed real enough. She set up a calendar to mark off the days to the Gaucho Cup, and from that to her next job, but that only made the black hole without Dante yawn in front of her like an unbridgeable chasm.

She managed a few hours of sleep before dawn. The scent of blossom was heavy in the air when she opened the window. Leaning out, she dragged in some greedy breaths—then shot back, seeing Dante in the yard. Even cloaked in shadows he was a stunning sight. She watched him prowl into the stable block and wondered why he was up so early. The urge to follow him, to find out where he was going proved to be one old habit that time hadn't dimmed.

Remembering the thrill of riding out with him at dawn

the day before, she tugged on her breeches as fast as she could, pulled her hair into a ponytail and dragged on a top and riding boots—then stilled, hearing the sound of hooves on cobbles. She smiled at the sound of Dante's husky whisper as he coaxed his horse to leave the prospect of an early feed in favour of the wide open spaces of the pampas. She'd catch him up—stalk him on horseback, as she had years ago.

She hurried downstairs and crossed the yard, heading for the stable block. Tacking up the same horse as yesterday, she led him out. Dante had a head's start but the sun was rising, showing her the way. She was confident she'd find him. She'd trust her instincts and those of a horse seeking out his stablemate.

She trailed him at a distance. Dante was riding at a steady pace, making it easy to keep him in sight. She had a small setback when the early morning sun went behind a cloud, and when it cleared again there was no sign of Dante. She looked about, searching for him, and then shrieked with alarm as strong arms scooped her from her horse.

'Now we talk,' he snarled as he lowered her to her feet in front of him.

'We're in the middle of nowhere!' She was still shocked, and angry that he had got the better of her.

'Exactly,' he agreed. 'No distractions.'

'You set this up?' She was trembling with fury—and something else she didn't care to analyse.

'I set you up,' he confirmed with a look.

Angling his stubble-shaded chin, he stared at her with all the old arrogance. She couldn't believe she'd fallen for it, but she had always been gullible where Dante was concerned.

It was as if the two of them were alone on a massive stage, with the strengthening sun dazzling her like a spotlight. All the early birdsong fell away as Dante's black stare drilled into hers.

His grip tightened on her arms. 'You've successfully avoided talking to me face to face for almost ten years. My best guess?' His black stare speared into her eyes. 'If you hadn't been forced into my company, you'd still be avoiding me. I'm giving you one last chance to tell me what you're hiding from me. And be warned, I won't ask again. I'll appoint investigators to find out the truth for me instead.'

She felt sick and faint. It had never occurred to her that Dante would go to those lengths. Dragging in a breath, she tried to remain calm, but the steel in his eyes and in his voice had thrown her.

'Why are you here, Karina? Why did you follow me?'

'I was curious,' she said with a shrug, in an attempt to make light of it. She had followed him because she had wanted to be close to him, she added silently.

'You're curious?' With a laugh, he shook his head. 'How do you think I feel about you?'

Dante's laughter was as cold as his stare. She should have listened to the gossip that said no one could reach out and touch Dante Baracca. Many had tried, but they had all given up. Only she was stubborn enough to believe that the man she had spent her teenage years dreaming about still existed.

'It's about that night, isn't it, Karina? It's something to do with that night.'

'Don't be silly,' she said defensively, desperate to change the subject.

'Tell me, Karina. Tell me every detail of what's happened to you between that night and this.'

'Why should I?' she stormed, lashing herself inwardly as she tried to skirt the truth.

'Because the woman standing in front of me is not the Karina Marcelos I used to know, and I demand to know why.'

'You demand?' she interrupted, laughing at the bitter irony of them both searching for something that didn't exist any more. 'The Karina Marcelos you mean no longer exists. She was a stupid—naïve—girl...'

Dante pulled his head back. 'What are you trying to say, Karina?'

She tried to breathe and could only suck in air in great gasps.

'Karina!' Dante all but shouted. 'Tell me what is wrong.'

Holding out her hand as if to fend him off, she somehow formed the words. 'You left me pregnant.'

Her voice sounded too loud, and the impact of her words shocked even Dante into silence. They stood together without moving, without breathing, without reacting at all, until he ground out, 'Why didn't you tell me this before?'

Her wounded gaze flashed to his. 'Because I'm not the person I was then.'

'You held this information from me?' He looked at her incredulously with eyes that had turned to steel—whether with fierce empathy or with fury, she couldn't tell. She could understand his shock and something of what he must be feeling, but she had no words to reach him.

'Don't you have anything to say to me?' His voice was harsh with frustration. 'Don't you think you at least owe me an explanation for your long silence?'

Her glance flashed to his hand on her arm and he let her go.

'What happened to our child, Karina?' he said. 'What happened to my baby?'

'There is no child.' Her voice sounded faint and far away. She was shaking so much she didn't recognise herself. She had imagined this scene so many times, and had even planned how she would phrase the words Dante must hear, but there were no words, she discovered now.

'Karina.'

She looked up to see Dante's expression had changed. Bringing her in front of him, he asked in a far gentler tone, 'Can you tell me what happened?'

'I lost the baby.'

She pressed her lips together as if that could stop it being true as silence swept over them again, holding them tight in its unfeeling grasp.

He wasn't sure how long they remained standing together, frozen and barely breathing as they stared at each other. 'You were pregnant,' he managed at last. All his anger and impatience with Karina had gone, leaving him feeling completely numb.

Her eyes searched his. 'I couldn't tell you, because you were away, and because—' Her mouth snapped closed again, and she shook her head as if it was too painful to go on. After a few moments had passed she drew a deep, shaking breath and continued. 'There were many reasons why I didn't get in touch with you, and by the time I saw you again it was over, and there didn't seem much point.'

'Much point?' he echoed softly, still trying to come to terms with what she'd told him.

'No point in upsetting you,' she explained.

He relaxed his grip on her arms and stood back. 'You

should have told me. You can't keep something like that to yourself. Who was there to help you?'

The answer was in her eyes.

'You told no one? Not even Luc? I would have been there for you if I'd known. I would have cancelled anything to be there for you.' It was a fight for him to keep rock solid as her eyes filled with tears. 'Yes, this has been a shock,' he admitted, 'and it would have been a shock then. I was younger. I was wild. But I was never uncaring. You should never have had to go through that alone.'

Actions had consequences, his conscience told him. This he knew, but what Karina had just told him was worse than anything he had imagined. How young she'd been—just eighteen. He'd been twenty-two—and reckless. But Karina had been alone with no one to confide in. Not that she would have done so anyway, he guessed grimly. She would hardly have told Luc, and if he had been around, *would* she have told him? Karina had always prided herself on standing on her own two feet, and she would have viewed explanations as a plea for help.

'I don't know what I could have done to help you,' he admitted. 'I was different back then—selfish and wild—and I know how independent you've always been, but I still can't believe you had to go through this on your own.'

She looked away and he knew he'd lost her.

'This was a mistake,' she said, confirming his fears. 'I shouldn't have told you. What's the point?'

'You're wrong,' he argued firmly. 'There's every point. What happened was my responsibility as much as yours.'

'No.' Her eyes blazed briefly. 'I don't need your counsel, Dante. I don't want you to feel sorry for me. I've told you everything you need to know. Now, please…don't mention it again.'

But had she told him everything? The look on her face, the flicker in her eyes told him she hadn't. 'Karina?'

'No,' she flared, pushing his hand away. 'I miscarried, something that happens to many women, the doctors told me.'

'Don't,' he warned quietly as her face turned grim and still. 'Don't try to dismiss this as if it means nothing to you, when I can see that it's breaking your heart.'

'I don't know what you're waiting for me to say,' she blazed.

The thought that there was more than this—more that she wouldn't tell him—tore him up inside. They'd been friends. They'd shared everything. And now, just when she needed someone, whether she knew it or not, Karina was turning her back on him.

'I know you,' he said quietly. 'I know that even at eighteen, if things had worked out and you'd had the child, you would have coped. As it was, you handled the tragedy and came through it alone.'

'Leave it, Dante,' she cried out. 'What's the point in this? I can't change anything—and neither can you!' she exclaimed with frustration. 'We just have to accept, you and I, that everything turned out for the best.'

'For the best?' he echoed over her. Now he knew something was badly wrong. 'I can't believe you just said that. This isn't the Karina I knew talking, and I refuse to believe you mean it.'

Sucking in a shuddering breath, she turned away. 'Can we please get back to business? We're wasting precious time talking about something neither of us can change.'

Her eyes were shuttered when she turned back to face

him. The subject was closed as far as Karina was concerned. But not for him.

'Back in Rio, you said my business acumen was all you wanted from me,' she reminded him. 'I hope that's still true.'

'You carried my child, Karina. That changes everything.'

She looked at him in silence for a few moments and then, returning to her horse without another word, she mounted up and rode away without a backward glance.

He needed to ride. He needed time to think so he could take in everything Karina had told him. She'd been pregnant and had kept that from him. He couldn't get his head around it. She'd lost the baby and had suffered that loss on her own. His guilt was like a living thing riding heavily on his back. The pampas had always been his outlet, a non-judgemental channel for his thoughts, but he doubted that even riding across the land he loved could bring him solace today.

He could never repair the past—never make up for not being with her when she'd lost a baby, their child, and had soldiered on unsupported. That was so typical of Karina—stubborn, dogged, brave and strong. She was like a cork, in that whatever life threw at her she always bobbed up. Luc had supplied all the necessities of life when she'd been growing up, including his unconditional love, but Luc had been too busy trying to find his own way to keep watch constantly over Karina. She wouldn't have listened to her older brother anyway.

He rode faster, as if that would give him the answer. When they had been kids, trust had been a simple matter of asking a question and receiving an honest answer.

They'd had no reason to lie to each other or to keep the truth from each other. Too much had happened for them to pick up the ease of those early days, but he had to do something because he knew for certain that there was more Karina wasn't telling him—and if that was as bad as what she had already told him…

His mood darkened as he considered the possibilities.

If he hadn't broken with her that night…

He'd had to break up with her. They had both been too young, too passionate, too unformed when it came to knowing who they were and what they wanted out of life. Sex had been an outlet for their energy and frustration, an impulse they had recklessly followed. Animal instinct had taken him over, as it must have gripped his father so many times. The break-up afterwards had been driven by his dread that one day he would become his father, and so he had pushed Karina away.

As the years had passed and he had matured and changed, he'd known for certain that he wasn't and never would be his father. That was why he'd opened up his home, and why he intended to do more of it, welcoming people of all ages to experience life on a working ranch. His childhood home would no longer be a place of fear and shadow but a home filled with happiness, purpose and light. He wanted Karina to experience the same redemption, but to do that she had to trust him first.

Karina was riding fast and hard in an attempt to forget that she had opened Pandora's box—to forget the past, to forget the present, to forget she'd told Dante about the baby—wishing with all her heart that she hadn't opened up, and yet glad that she had, and so glad that she'd retained the sliver of reason required to hold the rest of her secrets in. They were nothing to do with Dante. Why burden him?

For a while the concentration she required to ride at speed worked for her, but deep down the truth was burning, and Dante wouldn't let up now he suspected there was more.

Easing back in the saddle, she slowed her horse to give them both a much-needed break. Riding the pampas had always been healing, but what she'd been doing had been needlessly reckless. Her only excuse was that it had been too long since she'd ridden with the wind in her hair, and with the past driving her she'd gone all out.

Her horse responded happily to the change of pace with a high-stepping trot. It gave her the chance to look around and appreciate the countryside. The scent of herbs and grass beneath his hooves made her smile through her sadness. When had been the last time she'd taken the time to notice her surroundings? This dawn ride was such an evocative reminder of her childhood, when she had used to ride out with Dante, and it let a little optimism into her thinking.

She could see him in the strengthening light, riding in the distance, riding fast. They still had a lot of ground to cover. She understood that he had needed space after her revelations. He was doing what she had tried to do, which was to ride the sorrow out. Reining in, she watched him cut a path through the flatlands in a cloud of dust and thunder. At full stretch on horseback, Dante was a stunning sight. It was an image she'd always keep etched on her mind.

With a wistful smile, she sucked in a breath. This was Dante's home. At one time it had been her home too, but nothing stayed the same, and now her horse was chafing at the bit, impatient to be free. She knew how that felt.

'Okay,' she whispered, leaning low to reach his ears. 'Go get him!'

Her mount responded eagerly with a surge of speed that thrilled her as he set off after his stablemate.

Dante had reined in and he turned in the saddle when she trotted up alongside him. His expression was un-readable, and she tensed immediately, wondering what he was thinking now. She concluded the only thing she could do was break the ice.

'I'd forgotten how much I love it here.'

'The city didn't fulfil your expectations?' Dante que-ried, searching her eyes keenly.

'I thought it had until I came back here,' she admitted honestly. It was a struggle to keep everything except an open smile off her face. She gestured around to give her-self a moment. 'The city could never compete with this.'

She was putting on the act of her life. When Karina looked into his eyes he could see her pain, however hard she tried to hide it. He responded with a swell of emotion he had thought he was dead to. Underneath her bravado and her professional veneer Karina was the same girl he had known all those years ago, but she was wounded now.

'Is there any of the ranch left to see after our tour yes-terday?' she asked him brightly.

Some people might have expected more grief from her after the dreadful news she'd shared, but he knew Karina. He knew her strength, and now he knew her weakness. She had been keeping secrets for so long she didn't know how to share them. 'There's plenty left to see,' he told her truthfully. 'We'd better get on.'

He had to do something to help her, but there wasn't

time to do more than watch over her now. Her work had saved her, he guessed, just as Team Thunderbolt had saved him. The team had become his family, giving him a safe outlet for his youthful aggression.

The team had also given him back his sense of pride after his father had stripped it away, and a satisfaction in his work that his father had always denied him. Team members prided themselves on their loyalty to one another. If one of them hurt, they all hurt. If one of their loved ones hurt, there wasn't a team member who would stand by and do nothing. And this was Karina. How much more did he want to help her to reclaim the *joie de vivre* she had once enjoyed and spread around? But he could do nothing for her while she was keeping secrets. And no one knew better than he that Karina Marcelos had the strength to keep those secrets for the rest of her life if she chose to do so.

'Don't scowl, Dante.' She flashed him a look of concern. 'Life is full of twists and turns, and we just have to stay on our feet.' Closing her eyes, she demonstrated her intention to carry on with the job as if she wasn't breaking up inside. Throwing back her head, she murmured, 'It's such a beautiful day.'

He nodded curtly when she opened her eyes and turned to look at him. He was capable of nothing more in the face of her strength, because that was the same strength that was destroying her. Clicking his tongue, he led the way forward, hoping Karina would find some outlet for her trapped emotions in the beauty of the pampas so she could turn her back for good on shadow and doubt.

CHAPTER TEN

THEIR NEXT STOP was a group of buildings that could best be described as rustic rather than ritzy.

'This is the accommodation for visiting children, teachers and guardians,' Dante explained.

Now they were getting to it. She remembered Nicky's remark about Dante's plan, but why hadn't he been more forthcoming? If he needed long-term plans for the children it was going to be a much bigger job than she had bargained for—and in the time available he was stretching her to the limit.

'I think you'd better explain,' she said. 'Is this more than just about the Gaucho Cup? Because, if it is, I need to work out how I'm going to splice in your plans for an ongoing programme with my plans for the polo cup.'

'If you can't—'

'This isn't about my capabilities,' she interrupted. 'This is about you being frank with me, so I know what I have to do.'

'Me being frank with you?' he queried with a sceptical look.

'Yes.' She firmed her jaw. 'Either you want me to do this job or you don't.'

She held her ground as Dante stared at her. She guessed

no one, with the possible exception of his team members, stood up to Dante these days.

The standoff lasted a good few seconds, and then he grated out, 'Your job will be to enthuse the young people, draw them into the life of a working ranch. I'll give you all the plans I've drawn up so far.'

'Thank you. Gauchos,' she murmured, quickly summoning up in her mind the type of help she would need in the short a space of time available.

'Good idea,' Dante conceded, as she outlined her instinctive initial thoughts.

'Where to now?' she asked him briskly before he had chance to change his mind.

'To our last stop for today.'

She'd leave her questions about his long-term project for now. When time was squeezed it paid to be organised.

The last stop turned out to be the first ugly building she'd seen on his ranch.

'Vaults aren't meant to be pretty,' he said when she frowned. 'You might change your mind when you see the jewels inside this fortified cell.'

'Green ice,' she murmured, feeling a thrill of anticipation as Dante punched in a code and the outer door swung open. Lights flashed on automatically, illuminating the steps leading down into the ground. Another door, another code, and they were in.

The large underground room took her breath away. Glass cabinets, lit discreetly, lined the walls. It was a billionaire's showroom, alight with fabulous jewels. Diamonds and emeralds flashed fire on every side. She guessed the diamonds would be from the Skavanga mines Dante had talked about, and the combination of ice and fire was extraordinary. 'I'm lost for words,' she admitted, when Dante looked for a reaction from her.

'Well, that's inconvenient,' he said, locking the door behind them, 'because you're here to talk.'

She tensed as he leaned back against the wall.

Karina was smart. She knew why she was here, and it wasn't just to look at his priceless collection of jewels. She had never leaned on anyone in her life, not even her wealthy brother. She had no history of confiding in anyone, but he had a plan.

Unlocking one of the display cases, he reached for a rough diamond. 'This is me...' He placed the lump of unpromising-looking stone in her hand. 'And this is you.' He selected what looked like another pebble. 'Both these lumps of rock hold secrets at their core.'

'And you have to know how to release the secrets?' She gave him a jaundiced look. 'First you have to know what you're looking for,' she pointed out.

Never underestimate Karina, he reflected, slanting a smile as he replaced the stones in the cabinet. He explained the stages the stones went through before they were ready to be set in precious metal, but she knew what he was really saying. He had never brought anyone this close. He had never allowed himself the indulgence of a personal life. He didn't confide in anyone.

'Would it be possible to arrange tours here, as well as to the mine?' she asked on a practical note. 'Or would security be a headache for you? I wasn't just thinking about the VIPs who might place an order, but the young people for whom this could open up a whole new range of possibilities—careers,' she explained.

His eyes lit at the thought that she had engaged with his project. He'd barely told her anything, just a hint, but she'd taken that hint and had obviously been thinking about it. 'Your brother told me that you pay for a young girl to go to school.'

She was instantly defensive. 'Out of my own money—and Luc shouldn't have said anything.'

'It's nothing to be ashamed of.'

'No, but Jada wouldn't like anyone to know—that's the girl I help,' she explained awkwardly.

'How long have you been doing charity work?'

'Since I—' Her mouth snapped shut.

Since she'd lost the baby, he guessed, and had needed something to focus on and set her life back on track.

'It's not reaching out on your scale or my brother's,' she said after a few tense moments. 'I just do what I can afford. When I can do more, I will.'

Shaking his head, he disagreed. 'What you do is personal. I don't know the names of half the people helped by my foundation.'

She mulled that over for a moment, and then she said, 'So can I add tours here to the youth programme?'

'Over to you,' he agreed with a shrug.

It was a great idea. Opening young minds to careers connected to gemstones was original and pure Karina. It was maybe the first step to finding that fairy dust of hers. He held out a chair, leaving her in no doubt that he wasn't so distracted by her brainwave that he had forgotten why he'd brought her here. Her gaze darted to the door. He folded his arms and leaned back against the wall. Seeing there was no escape, she perched on the edge of the chair in fight or flight mode.

'Dante—'

Chair legs scraping across the floor silenced her. He

pulled up another seat and sat so their knees were almost touching.

Tension soared between them.

He let the silence hang until she said, 'Okay. What more do you want to know?'

'Everything,' he suggested. 'And, as you pointed out, the clock is ticking, and there's a lot of work to do to get this cup organised.'

'It isn't that easy,' she admitted. 'Some things can't be said quickly.'

'What can't you tell me? I can't believe there's anything worse than you've already told me.' Leaning close, he took hold of her hands.

She drew them back and balled them tightly in her lap. 'I can't. You chose your path. I chose mine—'

'That's not enough.' He stood.

She stood too, facing him defiantly. Anything was preferable, as far as he was concerned, to Karina in shutdown mode. 'Tell me,' he insisted fiercely.

The flash of pain behind her eyes said he was delving too deep, too fast, into places even she didn't go, but he couldn't let her go back into her shell now.

Emotion burned starkly in her white face. She knew there was nowhere to hide. She also knew he was the biggest client she'd ever have, and that her brother, not to mention the rest of the team, was depending on her to get this event right. She'd clawed her way to success, which was why people trusted her. He had to believe she wouldn't let that trust go now.

'Will you, please, let me out of here?'

He sensed she was holding herself tightly in check. 'You can leave at any time.' He recited the code for the door.

She sucked in a few tense breaths, and then she made

the decision he had fully expected. 'I'm not going anywhere, Dante, because you're right, that would be far too easy for me—for both of us.'

If this were the time she finally unburdened herself, he'd take anything she had to throw at him. His pride, his concerns, his life counted for nothing while Karina was in torment. And she was in torment. When she lifted her chin he could see the pain in her eyes and he felt it as his own. He had to tamp down the urge to drag her close and tell her that everything would be all right, and that he would make it so, because that would be a lie. This was something Karina had to do for herself.

He clenched his hands into fists as she drew in a long shaking breath. The urge to reach out was overwhelming him. But he mustn't touch her. He mustn't speak. If he did anything to distract her, this moment would be lost, and then she would be lost.

Closing her eyes tightly shut in a failed attempt to hold back her tears, she said, 'You do know if there'd been a child I would have told you?'

'Of course I do.'

'I was fine,' she lied, hurrying to reassure him. 'Life doesn't grind to a halt when a tragedy happens, and it's amazing how we find ways to cope.'

He clamped his lips shut as he raged against his inability to say anything that could make the slightest difference, and he felt even worse when she touched his arm as if it were he who needed comfort and reassurance.

'I'm sorry, Dante. I've had longer to adjust than you have.'

But she hadn't moved forward.

'I promise you this won't affect my work. I'll give

you everything I've got to make this the best polo cup there's ever been.'

His brain was racing as he searched for a way to shake her back on track. He needed something that would shock her into leaving the business between them to one side for now. She was hiding something bad, and this was his best—maybe his only—chance to help her. He barely heard the rest, and there was no way he could dress this up. A shock was needed, and a shock was what he'd give her.

'Did you take a lover after you lost the baby?'

Dante's question was like a slap in the face. Her mind blanked for a moment. She was still taking tiny steps. They had warned her in the hospital that it would take a long time to recover fully, and that in the meantime she would find coping strategies, but that no stage of her recovery could be rushed.

She had rushed. She would have done anything to ease the pain. At the time her actions had seemed to be the one thing that might help her to forget Dante. It had turned out to be her worst mistake, and had left her feeling more of a failure than ever.

'Well?' Dante pressed now, staring fiercely into her eyes. 'Are you going to answer my question?'

Desperate to close down this line of questioning, she shook her head. 'You can't ask me that.'

'I am asking,' he insisted grimly. 'I've listened carefully to everything you've said. I haven't missed a single nuance or hesitation in your speech, which is why I know there's more, and if it's something you can't talk about after what you've told me—if someone's hurt you physically, mentally, I want to know. And if you expect me to accept some lame excuse, you're dealing with the wrong man.'

'I've told you everything,' she insisted in a shaking voice. 'You can't hold yourself responsible for everything in my life. And you don't have a hold on me, so let me go.'

Breath gushed from her lungs as Dante dragged her close. 'If I live ten lives and devote them all to you, I will never make up for what happened to you, so if you think I'm going to let you go, let *this* go, you're mistaken.'

Guilt was careering through her when he dragged her close. She was shocked by his passion and should have remembered Dante had always channelled his emotion into action. A few blank seconds passed and then, like a dam breaking, her emotions flooded in as he drove his mouth down on hers. His kiss was like oxygen to her starved senses. The reassurance of his arms was like water in the desert to a dying man. It was too precious to squander, too welcome to ignore. For everything that had gone before and couldn't be changed, Dante was so instantly familiar. All fear of kissing him, of becoming close to him again seemed irrelevant suddenly. She was close to him. She had always been close to him—always would be close to him.

Lifting his head, he stared down. His black eyes were ablaze with inner torment as he grated out, 'I should have been there for you.'

Lifting herself up on her toes, she laced her fingers through his hair, and then she cupped his face, loving the scratch of his sharp black stubble against her palms. She wasn't a teenage temptress without a care in the world now, but a woman who knew her own mind. 'You're here now,' she whispered.

Dante's kisses changed and became lighter and more

reassuring, and then he did something that only he could. He started whispering things that no one else knew about them—small things, confidences they'd shared when they'd been younger, personal moments of triumph and defeat, times that hadn't been so good, and those that had been better, and times when a look between them had been enough to share the burden of what they had both been experiencing at home.

What he was trying to tell her was that nothing had changed between them, not really. He was reminding her of what they'd shared in the past, and reminding her that she'd never had cause to doubt him before that night when passion had run so high between them that neither of them had been thinking clearly.

She smiled into his eyes. She loved everything about him. She loved the way he made her feel, and the way he made her remember. She loved the way he soothed her, and the way he reminded her that they had faced tough times before and had always come through them. She loved the way he could make her smile when her heart was breaking, and she loved knowing that there was no-where else on earth she wanted to be than here, with him.

The need to be closer still overwhelmed her and, tugging his top from his jeans, she exclaimed with pleasure when her hands found his hot skin. Dante had started work on the buttons of her shirt, but he soon lost patience and ripped it off her, scattering buttons everywhere.

'What is this?'

Dante frowned as he stared at the scar on her shoulder.

'It's nothing.' Her head had cleared immediately as she shrugged it off.

Dante wasn't convinced. 'You didn't have a scar on

your shoulder when you were eighteen. I would have re-membered something like that.'

She shook her head and laughed, hoping to give the impression that he was making too much of it. 'If you must know, some insect bit me.' She huffed another laugh in the hope that he'd forget.

Dante didn't forget anything, and his frown deepened as he traced the scar with the pad of one finger.

'This is it, isn't it?' he said, lifting his head to stare into her eyes. 'This is your problem. Did someone do this to you? No,' he murmured after she had been silent for a while. 'It's worse than that, isn't it? Has someone intimidated you into silence, Karina?'

She wasn't looking for his pity. Everything she'd done in her life she'd done with her eyes wide open. 'Who's going to hurt me?' she scoffed. 'Have you forgotten I'm armour-plated?' She hastily pulled the remnants of her shirt back over her shoulders and crossed her arms over her chest to hold the two halves together.

Letting her go, Dante stood back as if he was disap-pointed. 'You will tell me eventually. But for now it's time we returned to our work.'

She wouldn't be so sure of that, Karina thought as he opened the door for her. She'd buried her secrets deep where not even Dante could find them.

CHAPTER ELEVEN

WHEN THEY GOT back to the ranch Dante dismounted and handed the reins of his horse to a waiting groom. She did the same. Unbuckling his leather chaps, Dante handed those over too. Down to snug-fitting jeans and a tight black top that moulded to his powerful body perfectly, he was a riveting sight, but he had become distant with her. She guessed her inability to confide in him had set their tenuous personal relationship back, and it was crucial now to restore communication between them.

She quickened her step to follow him across the perfectly manicured lawn. Everything inside the house was plain and good. There was no flash, no show. And no children, she discovered when they stepped inside. No staff either, by the look of things. Just the scent of freshly cut flowers and beeswax, contained with a heavy, but not oppressive silence.

'I've given everyone the day off,' Dante explained.

So they were alone. Had he planned this? She was instantly tense, imagining the interrogation she might face at any minute. 'What fabulous flower arrangements,' she commented, for want of something to say.

'It's the first thing I do each morning,' he said, turning to give her a look. 'Right after I muck out the horses.'

She relaxed into a laugh. Dante had always known how to reach out and touch her when no one else could.

'Coffee?' he said, heading for the kitchen. They had missed breakfast for the second day in a row.

They walked past the foot of the grand staircase, an elegant sweep of highly polished mahogany with a scarlet runner down the centre held by gleaming brass rods. There was a grand piano tucked neatly beneath the curve of it.

'You play?' she asked with surprise. The lid was up and there was music on the stand. 'Before you arrange the flowers, I'm guessing?'

Dante's tension also eased into a smile. 'I play whenever I get the chance,' he admitted. 'I just don't broadcast it.'

'The team would mock?' she suggested.

'They'd only do that once,' he commented dryly. 'My mother insisted I learn,' he explained in a rare moment of openness. 'She said it would relax me.'

'And does it?' She ran her fingers across the keys.

'It helps,' he said tersely, as the bell-like sounds faded into silence.

'You're full of surprises.'

'And you're not?' he challenged, flashing her a sharp look.

Her cheeks blazed red as the man who looked like a barbarian but who now turned out to have all the sensibilities of an aesthete continued to stare at her. Would the surprises never end where this new Dante Baracca was concerned? She was certainly getting to know him all over again.

'Before breakfast I have another idea, Karina.'

Thrown off balance, she hesitated. 'What idea?'

'I need to unwind,' Dante admitted as he rolled his powerful shoulders. 'You do too.'

Unwind how? She followed him across the hall and down a corridor into an impressive leisure facility where there were marble floors and glittering fountains, and beyond the fountains an enormous swimming pool. 'You want to have a swim?' she queried. The time issue made her frown as she asked the question, along with a far more personal concern.

'I thought we'd both have a swim,' Dante said, as he stared at her keenly.

And reveal her body? She froze with horror at the thought.

'You don't find it cold in here, do you?' he asked with surprise.

'I hope the water's warm,' she said, to excuse her involuntary shiver.

Dante frowned. 'You never used to care. You swim too well to feel the cold.'

She never used to have scars to worry about at the time he was talking about. Her body hadn't just failed her when it had come to carrying Dante's baby, it had failed her as a woman, and she had paid a heavy price for that. Seeking comfort in someone else's arms had seemed a solution, the means of forgetting Dante. Looking back, she realised her behaviour had been so out of character she must have had a breakdown. The doctors had been right. She should have sought professional help, rather than trying to go it alone. They'd warned her that her hormones would be raging for quite some time, but they hadn't explained how that would affect her. She blamed herself for losing the baby, and blamed herself again for everything that had happened afterwards.

'Take a shower,' Dante suggested, thankfully oblivious to these thoughts, 'and then join me in the pool.'

'I can't swim in jeans and a top.' She smiled back at him as she shrugged an apology.

'No problem. I keep a stock of swimsuits for my guests.'

'Maybe it isn't such a good idea.' Her alarm rose to fever pitch. 'I've got so much work to do—'

'And a swim first will allow you to clear your head.'

'I'd rather not.'

'Give yourself a break, Karina,' Dante insisted. 'Work is important to both of us, but we also need to take some downtime.'

She stared at him in silence for a moment, knowing there was no getting out of this.

From the selection of brand-new costumes still in their packets, which had obviously been chosen for women with far more style than she had, she selected a sports costume that covered up a lot more of her body than the flimsy bikinis on offer. There had been a time when she had raced Dante across the lake in freezing water, and had never cared about fashion, so he wouldn't be surprised to see her in such a modest costume. She might just get away with this if she was lucky.

Dante was slicing through the water by the time she came out of the changing room. His powerful body, so bronzed and muscular, was fully extended, and for a moment it was enough to stand and watch him swim. He had such an easy grace he barely made a ripple in the water. Her heart speeded up when, sensing her arrival, he stopped swimming and looked up. She stepped to the water's edge, in a hurry to dive in. The sooner her body was fully submerged, the sooner she could relax.

He felt rather than saw Karina enter the pool area.

Her choice of costume surprised him when there were
so many more attractive options to choose from, but he
shrugged it off. He stopped at the far end of the pool and
turned to see her framed in light. It was as if the rays of
the sun were attracted to her and had fired blue sparks
into her ebony hair.

It reminded him of the dozens of times when they'd
gone swimming in the lake, when he'd thought her wild
black hair looked like a thundercloud with lightning running through it. But then she set about taming it with re-
morseless resolve. He wanted to tell her not to tie it back,
but to let it cascade around her shoulders like a water
nymph. She should also take off that regulation costume
so she was completely naked. He doubted water nymphs
wore anything.

Feeling his stare, she stepped back into the shadows,
but not before he had seen the flush of awareness on her
cheeks. His body responded instantly. He wanted the
wild Karina he had made love to, the Karina who would
have chosen the most outrageous bikini in the bright-
est colour, and would have flaunted it to taunt him. Instead, a wounded woman was hiding in the shadows,
having picked out what she had obviously decided was
the drabbest choice of costume and the one least likely
to entice him.

He raised a hand in greeting, only for her to pull her
hair into an even tighter knot on top of her head. As sub-
liminal messages went, that one was clear enough. He
could look, but this water nymph wasn't for touching.

He swam towards her underwater. He wasn't a saint,
and the sight of Karina in a tight-fitting swimsuit, even
one as severe she had chosen, made full immersion of his
aroused body a practical necessity. The costume showed

off her voluptuous figure to perfection. He would have to be unconscious not to notice how good she looked.

He surfaced halfway down the pool to find her still fiddling with her hair. He didn't need any reminders of how glorious that hair had felt beneath his hands when he'd laced his fingers through its silky thickness. It pleased him to see that, in spite of her best efforts to achieve a severe look, soft tendrils were still escaping. He dipped his head beneath the water so she couldn't see him smile, and when he surfaced he was in time to watch her perform a perfect swallow dive. She swam to reach him, and it was a relief to see her face was almost free from tension by the time she reached him.

'Oh, that feels good!' she exclaimed.

He was tempted to catch her close, but he wanted to be sure she'd loosened up and was ready for that first.

'Race?' she challenged, to his surprise.

'Why not?' he agreed. 'Want a head start?'

She huffed with mock contempt and took off without him.

Catching up easily, he swam alongside her until the last couple of yards when he pulled ahead.

'You are so unfair,' she complained. 'You always do that.'

'And you always fall for it.'

She lifted herself clear of the water in a cloud of silver bubbles, and then, scooping water, she splashed it in his face.

'Like that, is it?' he threatened.

She laughed. Dipping her arm into the pool again, she thrashed it across the water, dousing him completely. He couldn't let a challenge like that go unopposed, and launching himself across the pool he brought her down beneath the surface with him.

She escaped like a seal, wriggling free from his arms with no difficulty at all—but not before he had felt a tantalising brush of her breasts against his arm and her heat all over him.

'You'll pay for that,' she threatened as they faced each other.

'I'd like to see you try!'

Diving down beneath the surface, she grabbed hold of his legs and tried to bring him under. He resisted her easily, and diving down with her he brought her to the surface, struggling furiously in his arms. If there was a more erotic experience than having a hot, wet Karina fighting him off, he had yet to experience it. When he finally subdued her, she was laughing. 'You have to let me go,' she protested.

'Why, when this is much more fun?'

'For you.'

'For both of us.'

She saw the change in his expression and grew still. Winding his fist through her hair, he drew her head back slowly and then, taking his time so he could savour every moment of it, he brought his lips down on hers.

Hot and cold, wet and warm, the dark secrets of her body were yielding themselves up to him. He plundered her mouth with his tongue, mimicking the sex act he craved—the act that had gone on all night the first time. He could never forget how wild she'd been, how responsive, how abandoned. He could still remember her screams of pleasure and the way she had called out his name at the moment of release.

Karina had been insatiable and so had he. Bringing a premature end to that glorious encounter had been torture for both of them. They had discovered a capacity for pleasure he guessed neither of them had previously suspected. She was sucking his tongue now as she had sucked him that night…and now she was biting his bottom lip, just as she had teased and tormented him. She'd rubbed her warm breasts against him in open invitation as she'd wrapped her limbs around his, making him her captive, as he had gladly been that night—until he'd turned her beneath him to show her the meaning of deep, thrusting, rhythmical pleasure. She had responded by pressing her legs as far apart as far as she could, in order to isolate that most sensitive place for his attention. She'd cried and groaned and panted out her need, and as he pressed his erection into her now, he could feel the soft swollen warmth of her core yielding against him, just as it had that night. Her lips were wet, her mouth was hot, and he was as sure as he had ever been that Karina in her confining swimsuit was ready for him to take, to pleasure, to satisfy—

'No!'

She reeled away from him in the water as he began to ease her swimsuit down and quickly backpedalled in the water as if her life depended on putting distance between them.

'You stay in,' she insisted, reaching for a towel before she had even climbed out of the pool.

He sprang out to join her, shocked by her sudden change of mood—perplexed as she backed away, as if he were a threat in some way.

'What now?' she asked him warily, still backing away.

He shrugged in an attempt to ease the rigid tension between them.

'Now we get a massage,' he said casually, looping a towel around his waist.

She gave a nervous laugh, clearly unsure of his motive. 'You have masseurs on tap?'

'I have a phone. I'll take a shower and meet you by the massage tables.'

Her eyes widened. 'You have massage tables?'

'I have a gym with tables at the far end,' he said a trifle wearily, but she'd become so tense and serious he had to try and lighten things up. 'What type of place do you think I run here?'

'I… I don't know. If I believed your press—'

'Don't believe my press,' he warned.

'Y-you seem to forget I've got a b-brother,' she stammered.

'And?'

'And until Luc got married I wouldn't have put anything past him.'

He huffed a dry laugh. 'Getting married certainly slows a man down.'

She took a moment and then visibly recovered. Drawing herself up, she said, 'I don't expect that's anything you have to worry about.'

He shrugged, 'Your brother's a greatly changed man—and for the better, in my opinion.'

She had to agree with that. Luc had made a good choice of wife, and Emma had no trouble putting up with him, by all accounts.

'I've never seen my brother so happy,' Karina confirmed. 'Emma's been good for him, but the two of you are so similar I don't know how she puts up with him.'

'I don't know what you mean.'

'Use your imagination,' she suggested.

That was a very dangerous idea where Karina was concerned.

CHAPTER TWELVE

KARINA WAS SHOWERING, feeling tense, tracing her scars as she thought about Dante naked in the shower stall next to her. Every part of her was tingling and aware, but her emotions were in turmoil. She couldn't let him touch her again. It had raised the ghosts of the past and stirred them up into a shrieking frenzy. She should never have agreed to this.

What made it even more poignant, more painful was that on the night of her eighteenth birthday it hadn't been all about sex. There had been quiet times when they had lain naked on the bed, staring into each other's eyes, when she had believed they had never been closer. She'd been so naïve, imagining that making love with Dante meant they'd stay together for ever, and now here she was, blundering into another emotion-fuelled mistake.

She stilled as he turned off the shower.

'I'll be waiting for you outside, Karina.'

'Okay.'

Turning off the water, she reached for a towel. Confident he'd left the changing room, she stepped out of her own shower stall to find Dante just a few feet away. In the split second it took her to realise that he had his back turned and couldn't see her scars, ice shot through her.

Her heart lurched a second time. There weren't many men with a back view as good as their front, but Dante was one of them. He had a towel slung around his waist and was dripping water everywhere as he eased his powerful shoulder muscles in a gesture she was all too familiar with.

She stiffened as he turned to look at her.

Without losing eye contact, she reached blindly for another towel. He frowned as she wrapped it tightly around her. 'No need for that, Karina. The masseur's waiting for you.'

No point?

She made a disappointed face. 'I'm afraid I really have to take a rain check—not that I don't appreciate the offer of a massage, but by the time I dry my hair—'

'You're coming with me,' he said firmly.

Dante took hold of her arm to guide her out of the changing rooms, but she pulled back.

'What are you frightened of, Karina?'

'Nothing.'

He stared at her for a moment. 'Five more minutes to dry your hair and then I'm coming back for you.'

When he'd gone she stared in the mirror at her rabbit-in-the-headlights face. She couldn't keep running like this for ever.

'Where do I go for this massage?' she asked, when she came out of the changing room.

Barefoot, but dressed in jeans and a black top that emphasised his powerful physique, Dante led the way to the far end of the gym, where a luxurious sunken area had been designed to induce peace and relaxation. There were comfortable sofas and massage beds arranged around a decorative fountain; the scent of essential oils fragranced the air.

'Shall I lie down here and wait? You don't need to stay with me...'

Her voice was shaking and she realised she had backed up against one of the comfortable beds. The frame was jabbing into her lower back.

'What are you doing?' she exclaimed as Dante tried to take one of her towels away.

'You can't have a massage while you're wrapped up like a mummy,' he pointed out.

'I'm sure the masseur will tell me when to lose them,' she protested, taking a step to one side.

She frowned as she watched Dante pick out a bottle of massage oil from the selection on the shelf. 'Shouldn't we wait for the masseur to do that?'

And then the penny dropped. Dante had no intention of calling a masseur.

Bolts of alarm stabbed at her chest. She couldn't do this. She had gone along with it up to now to allay his suspicions, but this was as far as she could go. It had to stop.

'Get on the couch, Karina.'

Her mind was racing as she tried to find a way out of her predicament.

'Okay,' she agreed finally. 'But we do this my way.'

Dante's stare was dark and amused. That was how she planned for it to stay.

'This starts with you,' she said firmly.

His brow creased as he looked at her, and then his lips pressed down with amusement. 'I have absolutely no objection to being dominated.'

'Good,' she said lightly. 'Now we've got that settled, would you like to undress and lie down?'

All that was left was for her to instruct her heart to continue beating and breath to enter her lungs.

Dante had absolutely no worries about exposing his body to her and Karina hid her blush as he deftly stripped off his shirt and jeans. Turning towards the robes she'd noticed hanging nearby, she grabbed one and put it on over her towels before dropping them to the floor. Dumping them in a wicker basket marked 'Laundry', she belted her robe and an oil to use on Dante, choosing sandalwood—sultry, spicy and perfect for him. Warming it between her palms, she tried not to let her gaze linger on his powerful body, which was now stretched face down on the couch, awaiting her attention.

He shifted position impatiently. 'When you're ready…'

'I thought this was supposed to be our chance to relax? What's your hurry?'

'We've both got work to do,' he growled.

'Thank you for reminding me,' she said dryly, and with a deep breath she began, but not before she'd draped a towel over his taut buttocks. If she couldn't see them she would be able to resist feeling them beneath her hands!

Dante tensed the moment her hands touched him. She hadn't expected that. She hadn't expected the muscle memory in her fingers to hold such an acute recollection of the play of muscle beneath his skin. Her breathing quickened when he groaned with pleasure. She was obviously doing something right. Applying more pressure, she allowed herself to enjoy his silky heat. His body was hard and muscular, and there were sinister ink whorls on his powerful back and on his biceps. The staggering width and strength in his shoulders, tapering to a lean waist, reminded her how she'd felt when he'd loomed over her.

He was built to scale, she remembered, her mind going

back to that night. Thinking about such things was easy and safe, but actually *doing* anything like that again was another story; a story that was lost in the darkest part of her mind…

'Giving up already?' he demanded.

She swallowed convulsively, caught in the act of an extremely erotic thought. 'Of course not.'

She grew in confidence and Dante relaxed. Leaning over him, she threw all her weight into the massage, kneading his knotted muscles until they softened. She had plenty of time to think about the man she was getting to know all over again. Before she'd come to his ranch she'd had a vague idea that he would live in solitary splendour with an army of servants to do his bidding, when now she knew that nothing could be further from the truth—

'Is that it?'

She was startled to find Dante sitting up and staring her in the face.

He shrugged and swung off the couch when she didn't reply, tucking the towel she'd covered him with around his waist. 'Your turn now,' he said.

She flinched back as he stripped away the linen sheet he'd been lying on and replaced it with a clean one. 'Well?' he prompted. 'What are you waiting for?'

She couldn't move. She was filled with dread, but if she made him wait he would become more suspicious than ever. If she did as he asked, he'd see what she had been trying to hide from him.

She'd gone too far to get out of it, she decided, and her back was a safe zone. Unbelting her robe and slipping it down her shoulders she climbed up on the table and made sure she was lying on her stomach. Nervously, she waited—and tensed when Dante moved the robe down further but still covering her buttocks.

She relaxed as much as she could—which wasn't much at all—and remained on full alert when he moved away. She couldn't see what he was doing and the anticipation was killing her. The first touch of his hands nearly sent her into orbit. It delivered shockwaves to every part of her body. Her nipples pebbled, her breath quickened, and her body moistened, though she had contracted like a sea urchin flinching from a touch.

Sensing she was super-wired, he soothed her with long, firm strokes. Dante had always been the master of pleasure, and he knew just which muscles to work. He began at her shoulders and worked his way down her body with wicked skill. She was annoyed with herself for responding so eagerly, but all it took was a few short minutes and it was as if his hands had lifted the tension out of her, allowing her body to respond and soften, allowing her troubled mind to forget. Turning her face into the sun-bleached sheet, she inhaled deeply as she allowed herself to enjoy the experience of having Dante work her body. It was impossible not to progress her thoughts to that other night, and that deeper pleasure when she'd been in heaven, or somewhere very close.

When he stopped she almost cried out with disappointment, and only relaxed when he drizzled more oil on her back. The oil was warm and Dante's touch was soothing, and very soon the last of her tension had seeped away. Turning her head, she risked a glance at him, and saw the warmth and humour in his eyes.

Humour had always been her undoing where Dante was concerned. It was his most lethal weapon. She turned her face back into the sheet again, smiling. Humour was personal between them. It brought them close, and had done since they'd been young. She thought again about the night of the party, when Dante and her brother's friends had teased her as a matter of course. She'd given back as good as she'd got, accusing them of being more use to a horse than a woman and then not much use at all. They had laughed and drifted away...all except Dante.

'Don't you trust me, Karina?'

'Sorry?' She was confused for a moment as the past and the present clashed.

'I asked you to turn over,' he repeated.

'Onto my back?' The consequences of doing so destroyed her relaxation at a stroke.

'Unless there's another side of you I don't know about?' Dante murmured to himself.

Grabbing for the towel he presented her with, she covered herself and sat up. 'That was great. Thanks. But I'm done.' She was already swinging off the table. 'I need another shower,' she explained. 'I'm covered in oil—'

Breath rushed out of her as Dante scooped her off the couch.

'Where are you taking me?'

'Where I should have taken you from the start.'

He was striding down the gym. Panic overwhelmed her and she stiffened like a board. A surprised breath shot out of her when he set her down outside the door. Balling his hands into fists, he slammed them into the wall on either side of her face.

'What's wrong with you, Karina?' he gritted out.

Apart from her longing for shadows to hide in, or a door to slip through, did he mean? All out of options, she turned her face away from his.

'Don't hide from me,' Dante ground out, and cupping her chin he forced her to look at him.

'What's wrong with *you*, Dante? Do you find it so hard to believe that there's a woman in this world who can resist you?'

'You know that this has nothing to do with sex.'

'Do I?'

'And if it were, is that so terrible? I've seen the way you look at me. Either you're lying to yourself or you have a problem, Karina. Which is it?'

Firming her lips, she refused to speak.

Letting her go with a frustrated sigh, he stood back. 'I give up. Get dressed.'

Pulling away from him, she stalked angrily back to the changing room, where she found her clothes and tugged them on. She didn't care about her appearance or her hair. She just wanted to get away—away from Dante and his scrutiny, and his questions.

But he was waiting for her on the other side of the door. Slouched on one hip with his hands dug into his pockets, he leaned back against the wall. 'Before this project forced you out of the shadows, you were hiding away in your brother's hotel.'

'Hardly hiding,' she argued. 'I was working for my living.'

'Living life vicariously,' he continued, as if she hadn't said a word. 'Arranging other people's big occasions. Making other people happy, and making a name for yourself into the bargain. I think that was a side benefit you hadn't expected.'

'Any more words of wisdom or can I go?' Drawing herself up, she looked past him.

'You do a good job, I don't deny it,' Dante continued

unperturbed, 'but the fact that you were *so* good brought you to everyone's attention, which I imagine was the last thing you had in mind—especially when it brought you to *my* attention.'

'You are one arrogant—'

'You have a gift for organisation,' he said, talking over her in a low, intense voice. 'You cast your fairy dust on every party or event, but then your carefully constructed house of cards came crashing down when I walked back into your life. You couldn't ignore your secrets then, could you, Karina? For years you've done everything you could to avoid me, but now I'm back. The one person you should have confided in is back, and you won't get away with silence now.'

Huffing out a frustrated breath, she shook her head firmly. 'I have nothing to tell you.'

'You're a liar.' He pushed his face into hers. 'You never used to be a liar, Karina. So, what's happened to change you?'

'You,' she said icily. Her passion had soared way past the danger level, and caution had gone out of the window as they confronted each other unblinking. 'You think you know so much about me—but did you also know that I was a virgin that night?'

'Deus!'

She had the satisfaction of seeing Dante's look of horror, but little else. She was ashamed of herself for telling him that way. She had never meant to use it as a weapon, and on her birthday night she hadn't wanted to stop him. She had wanted to go the whole way with Dante, and had set out to do just that. Dante hadn't taken advantage of her. She had taken advantage of him.

'If this is this the truth, Karina, why didn't you tell me?'

'Why didn't you ask?'

'You—' Dante broke off to rake his hair in the familiar gesture that made her feel guiltier than ever, for springing something else on him that he couldn't possibly have known. 'Why, Karina?' His eyes were black with emotion.

'I thought you'd laugh at me if I told you.'

'Laugh at you?' he demanded incredulously.

'We didn't have that type of relationship. We were friends. I was a tomboy—one of the gang. You were always bragging about your conquests, all of you.'

He gave a short laugh. 'I didn't make love to you because you were one of the gang.'

'We were both wild that night—reckless.' Her mouth dried as she remembered. 'That's how we were—how you expected me to be. I didn't want you to think I was…soft.'

'It isn't soft to be a virgin. It's a life choice, and one some people stick to because it suits them.'

Shaking her head, she disagreed. 'Don't make me out to be some sort of saint when I was stupid and naïve. I wanted you. I wanted a magical end to my birthday. I didn't think any further than that. And it was special—for me at least. It was everything I'd ever dreamed of and so much more. But then you sent me from your bed and I was devastated. How do you think I can trust you now?'

'I made a mistake,' Dante admitted. 'You were savvy and smart, and we moved with the same wild group. You seemed to know it all. You were so beautiful that night and I wanted you. There seemed no point in waiting once you made it clear that you felt the same.'

'If you'd known I was a virgin, would it have made a difference?'

'Honestly?' His lips pressed down as he thought about

it. 'No, not if that was what you had wanted. But I would have been more careful with you.'

He groaned as he thought back to a night of hot, hungry passion when a go-slow had never been on the cards. 'I wanted you for all the wrong reasons. You were like a flame, drawing every man at the party towards your heat, and I had to have you. I had to claim you to show everyone you were mine.'

'And then you had to discard me?'

'And then I came to my senses,' he argued. 'I tried to save you from myself—a man who was nowhere near ready to settle down. I know you were trying to pretend you were someone else that night, and you're doing it again. You won't tell me what's hurt you, because you think you can tough it out on your own. How's that been going for you so far, Karina?'

'Let it go, Dante. Our lives have moved on.'

He shook his head. 'You carried my child. You're my friend—or you used to be. You're Luc's sister. Choose any reason you like, but that makes you my concern whether you want to be or not. You can't hold this poison inside you for ever or it will rot you from the inside out.'

'Let the past be!' she exclaimed. 'I don't need anyone to rescue me, especially not you. I've done okay and I'll do even better in the future. Yes, I was wild and, yes, I got pregnant, but when I lost my baby I knew my wild days were over for good, and there was only one way back, which was to have a purpose in life. Only then could I find my way forward again. You're wrong about me hiding away in Luc's hotel. I went after a career with the same single-minded determination that I went after you that night.' She dashed her tears away impatiently.

'And if our baby had lived, I would have done everything I could to be a good mother.'

'You don't have to convince me. I know that's true. But we're talking about then, and this is now, Karina. Let me help you. It's not a sign of weakness to reach out, and if you're in trouble, please, trust me enough to help you make it right.'

'You can't,' she said flatly, withdrawing like a wounded animal into her burrow.

'*Deus*, Karina! How are we going to work together if we can't communicate on any level?'

'This conversation has nothing to do with my work, and my personal life has nothing to do with you.'

'It has everything to do with me,' Dante argued fiercely. 'If someone I care about hurts, I won't turn my back on them.'

She shook her head and stubbornly refused to change her mind. 'In my case you'll have to make an exception.'

CHAPTER THIRTEEN

SHE GLANCED LONGINGLY towards the ranch house.

'Yes, you should go,' Dante agreed. 'Why don't you just give up and go home? I'm sure you can find a replacement to organise the polo cup.' He shook his head with annoyance.

Karina was annoyed with herself. Luc had taught her not to be a victim. Her brother had instilled in her the necessity for a spine of steel. Was walking out now the way to repay him?

'I'm not going anywhere until I've finished this job,' she said firmly.

Dante shook his head. 'It's not that easy, Karina. That decision is no longer yours to make. Either you tell me what you're hiding or you can leave.'

'You're threatening me?'

Dante remained silent.

'I have one week left. In that time I'll draw up my initial plans. The rest I can do from Rio. I'll tell you everything you want to know—'

'When will that be?' Dante asked harshly. 'Will you tell me to my face? Or will you text me on your way home? Perhaps you'll remember to send me an email when you get back to the safety of Rio. Why should I believe anything you say, when you stun me with the news that you were a virgin that night—horrify me with the fact that you lost our baby, and then hold back on this? You're not a woman I recognise, Karina. You've become a stranger to me.'

Stung and shocked by Dante's coldness, she fired back at him, 'And you're a man without a heart—a man who pushes everyone away except strangers, because they never get too close, do they, Dante? You bring people to your ranch and do so much good work on the projects, but by your own admission you don't know the name of a single person you help. You're more damaged than I am. You were hurt as a child and you still bear the scars of your father's contempt. You shy away from relationships. You're frightened of love. You're frightened to lay yourself open to hurt again.'

'I'm not frightened of anything!' His laughter was cruel as if he meant to hurt her.

'Prove it!' she challenged.

Driving his mouth down on hers, he did exactly that, kissing every rational thought from her head. Numb with shock for a moment, she felt his need as her own and kissed him back. Matching his passion, she fuelled it, knowing she had driven him to this. They had driven each other to the extremes of what it was possible for either of them to withstand.

And Dante's wasn't gentle with her, or playful, as he had been in the swimming pool. His kiss was the kiss of a man on the edge. She might have secrets but he had a whole world of hurt and bitter confusion inside him. Deep in his emotional core Dante Baracca, the hero of so many, was still trying to make sense of what he could have done to make his father hate him.

She knew the answer. He'd done nothing wrong. Dante thought no one knew, but people talked, and as a child she'd heard how he'd saved his mother from his father's violence, which had been the noblest, bravest thing a son could do. Dante had surpassed his father in every way, and that was his only fault. He'd had rebuilt his life as well as the family ranch where so many people came to explore new possibilities. She ached for him and cried for him, and for everything they'd lost.

He tasted salt on her lips and knew without doubt that for all her complex, stubborn ways there was no other woman on earth like Karina. She infuriated him, she frustrated him beyond measure but, then, she always had. There was only one Karina, only one woman who knew what made him tick. She knew his strengths and the weakness he never showed the world. She knew everything about him. He didn't have to explain his past.

There had been times when a sympathetic glance, or a brush of the hand, had been all that had been needed for two young people to acknowledge what had been going on at home, and it had helped them to know they hadn't been alone, and now it was enough to be together. Being with Karina was so natural it was like *coming* home, and even better when the pace of his kisses slowed and gentled and she softened in his arms.

There had been times when she had doubted they could ever recapture the closeness they had known, but now... She gasped with pleasure as Dante feathered kisses down her neck, and moaned softly when he rasped his stubble against her skin. The sensation transferred to every part of her, making her yearn, making her moist, and making her thrill with excitement, knowing she could feel normal again. With Dante it seemed that anything was possible.

'We've got all the time in the world,' he murmured as she tightened her hold on him. 'There's no rush, Karina.'

But she was in a rush to prove there was nothing wrong with her, and pressing against him she shivered with desire as his mouth brushed her ear, her cheek, her lips...

'Are you cold?' he asked, when she shivered.

She laughed softly. 'Anything but.'

He smiled into her eyes. 'And you trust me?'

He kept on kissing her as he led her back into the house, and in between those kisses he whispered outrageous suggestions that made her laugh, that made her lust, that made her believe they could pick up where they'd left off. He told her she made him happy. He made her smile. The closeness she had once taken for granted, and which had proved so elusive as they'd grown up, seemed to have returned.

They were still laughing when they reached the foot of the staircase—faces close, arms entwined, gazes locked on each other. She had never felt closer to another human in her life than she felt to Dante. And now he began to remind her of all the tricks she had used to play on him—innocent times before life and all its difficulties had caught up with them. The warmth they'd known had returned full force, she thought as he took her up the stairs. She was so lost in laughter and good memories she barely noticed crossing the threshold into his room.

'Don't pull back now,' he joked, not realising she was serious.

Her gaze darted about, taking in her masculine surroundings. An enormous bed filled her vision. She was transfixed by it as Dante took hold of her hand.

'Is there a problem?' he murmured, smiling down into her eyes.

'No. Of course not,' she said tensely. She flashed a smile meant to reassure him, and then he kissed her again and she wondered what she had been worried about.

'I'm going to make love to you—really make love to you,' he promised, as he steered her across the room. 'I want to make up for lost time.'

Dante was happy—confident—confident in her and her response, but she was already tense at the thought that he wouldn't want her when he knew.

'I'm sorry—'

Pulling back his head, he stared down at her in surprise. 'What do you have to be sorry about?'

So much she didn't know where to begin.

Lifting her into his arms, he carried her to the bed and she stared into the face she had loved since she was a child. This was right, this was good, she told herself firmly. She was a healthy female, and every part of her body was responding to Dante as it should. Nothing could go wrong this time.

When he lowered her to the floor at the side of the bed she reached out to free his top from the waistband of his jeans. Hooking his thumb into the back of the neck, he brought the top over his head, displaying the beautiful torso the cameras loved almost as much as she did. She would never get used to the sight of Dante naked. He was breathtaking. His stare on her face was dark and certain. He didn't need to tell her that he wanted her when she could see it in his eyes, and knew he would see the same in her own.

But would her body allow this?

'Karina?'

Sensing her abstraction, Dante clasped her shoulders to bring her back into the moment. She smiled up at him, though not before an involuntary swallow on a dry throat had gripped her. She could do this, she told herself again. She kept her gaze steady on his face to prove that she could—to him and to her.

'If you have any doubts...'

'I don't,' she insisted. This was Dante, and nothing was going to spoil it for her. Dante and Karina. Karina and Dante. Fate had always meant them to be together.

Tracing the broad sweep of his shoulders with her hands, she leaned forward to kiss his chest. Dragging greedily on his familiar clean, musky scent, she kissed him again. She wanted him to know how committed she was to this. She wanted him to know that this was quite different from the last time when her virginity had been hidden from him. Turning her face up to his, she stared him in the eyes and saw everything she'd hoped to see. Even the fact that Dante was so obviously holding back made her want him all the more. Her body was hungry for him and in no mood to wait. Moving restlessly against him, she closed her eyes, shutting out the last of her doubts.

She stiffened a little when he took off her bra, and then reminded herself that she was hidden in the dark. And then he touched her and the pleasure was extreme. When he cupped her breasts she groaned with pleasure and forgot everything but Dante's touch. It sent sensation streaming through her, and, more than physical, the way he touched her plumbed her emotions, making tears spring to her eyes. They were together, and that was all that mattered. They could never make up for what they'd lost, but they could start again.

Lowering her onto the bed, he lay down beside her. She was his, body and soul. Stretching out his length against hers, he smiled into her eyes. His face was inches away and in shadow, but she could sense the warmth in his face and hear his certainty in his steady breathing. He could seduce her just by being close, she mused wryly.

Reaching down, she found his belt buckle and freed it, and then she lowered the zip, her hand brushing the hard proof of his desire. Far from being intimidating, she longed to have him inside her.

No fear at all? How long would that last?

It would be all right. She would make it right. They were discovering each other all over again, only now they were old enough to commit on a deeper level. There wasn't a part of her that didn't crave Dante's touch, a part of her that didn't crave his love. He would never hurt her. Nothing could hurt her now.

He was devoted to Karina and to her pleasure. Whatever else he had expected today, it hadn't been this complete and welcome reversal into the girl he remembered, the girl who had used to be such a big part of his life. There was only one Karina. Even when she had avoided him, his hungry gaze had sought her out at every match. He'd got into the habit of scanning the crowd at polo matches, knowing he wouldn't play his best unless Karina was watching. He had never had the chance to tell her that she was his lodestone, his totem, and that when he had needed a reality check only Karina could challenge him and bring him down to earth. He'd missed that. He'd missed her. He'd missed the woman who could push her own concerns aside so she could help everyone else.

He'd been determined to have her the night of her party—determined to keep her, until things had gone so badly wrong. His callous behaviour had split them apart like a thunderbolt, forging a chasm between them and leading to tragic consequences.

Consequences Karina had been forced to go through alone.

'Dante?'

She had brought the sheet up to her chin, and was clinging to it like a comfort blanket. He eased down the bed to reassure her. He kissed and caressed her until she relaxed. He didn't need to test her to know that she was ready, but he wasn't taking a single chance this time. She cried out with pleasure at his intimate touch when he plundered her lush folds. She was soft and moist and swollen, and so ready for him that when he traced a finger lightly over her, she clung to him, gasping with need.

He protected them both. His aim was simple. He wanted to make up for that night. He wanted to hear her sigh with pleasure in his arms, and he wanted to take his time getting her to that place. But Karina didn't want to wait. It was almost as if she had something to prove—to him, to herself, he wasn't sure which. He only knew that she was responding with such fierce need it was sending him crazy with desire for her. But still he made himself wait. After everything she'd been through, caring for Karina was his only concern. It was his test, his trial by fire, and he would come through for her.

'I want you, Dante.'

'I know you do.'

She was still clinging to the sheet, but he understood

her modesty. She was even more beautiful than he remembered, and he found her vulnerability endearing.

She writhed with pleasure on the cool, crisp sheets, while Dante's hands worked their magic on her body. She was gaining in confidence every moment as he intensified her pleasure. There were no doubts left. She was as normal as any other woman. Dante had led her to a place of exquisite pleasure, and everything he did proved his care for her.

Throwing back her arms in an attitude of absolute trust, she held his stare as he moved over her. She sucked in one sharp breath when he teased her with the tip or his arousal, but then he did no more than draw it back and forth, which felt so incredible. She wanted him so badly she was aching for him and, acting on instinct, she arched up to claim him, but the instant he dipped inside her she pulled back.

'Karina?'

'I can't! Stop! Please… *Stop!*'

Tears of shame and failure sprang to her eyes as she pressed her hands against his chest in an attempt to push him away.

CHAPTER FOURTEEN

IT WAS A reflex action. She couldn't have stopped herself pushing Dante away if she'd tried. She had thought she was cured, that Dante had cured her, but her fear of love-making was instinctive. She had failed. She was broken. There was no cure.

She wasn't sure what she had expected from him, but it wasn't this. Dante had caught her tightly in his arms and he was holding her as if he had pulled her back from an abyss. Softening his grip, he brought her close and held her like a baby, but when he spoke his voice was firm. 'No more lies, Karina. I know I haven't done this to you, so who has?'

There was no going back now. Even if the truth drove him away, she had no option but to tell him. Sucking in a shuddering breath, she picked through her mangled thoughts in an attempt to make sense of the incomprehensible. Her fear was real, but irrational, and she had never spoken of it out loud before. 'After I lost—'

'I know that part,' Dante whispered, as he stroked her hair. 'Take your time.'

She did as he said and took longer to pull herself together. 'I had to rebuild my life,' she said then. 'A life I believed you were no longer part of.'

'And with good reason,' he agreed.

'While I was recovering, I knew I could do one of two things. I could retreat from the world or I could get back in the saddle and take another tilt at it.'

'And you decided to get back in the saddle.'

'Yes, I did. But then I discovered that moving too fast is not a good thing when your life is in turmoil. My judgement was off. Going away to college was the right thing to do. I made some good friends, and I found something I had a flair for. If I'd left it there and come home after my course, everything would have been okay, but I was too needy—'

'You were vulnerable,' Dante argued.

'Don't make excuses for me.' She pulled the sheet tight. 'I stayed on, and then there were complications…' She stopped and frowned.

'Go on,' Dante prompted.

'There was a man—one of my college tutors.'

'Older than you?'

'Much older,' she confirmed. 'But I was mature enough to know what I was doing.'

'You'd lost a baby. You were alone.'

'My head was all over the place, but because things had gone so well with the course and my friends it was easy to persuade myself I was ready for everything else—a new relationship, for example… Someone to help me get over you.'

'You were looking for reassurance, which is hardly surprising,' Dante agreed.

'Don't try to make me feel better. Everything that happened was my fault.'

He shrugged. 'I can't comment. You haven't told me what happened yet.'

'I'm not going to pretend to you. I was like a ship without an anchor and for a short time this man made me feel safe.'

Now she saw the expression she had expected to see on Dante's face: the face from the posters, a face turned grim; a man no one crossed, unless they had a death wish.

'He made you feel safe because you had no one else to confide in, and he took advantage of that fact. This happened, not because of something you did.' Dante's face blackened. 'It happened because I wasn't there for you when you lost the baby.'

'No.' She shook her head decisively. 'I was weak. And it ended badly,' she added. 'And you don't need to hear the rest.'

'You can't stop now, Karina.'

As Dante's black eyes blazed into hers she knew he was right. Inhaling raggedly, she told him the rest of it. 'I thought I could forget you if I was with someone else. I thought I could forget that night and start over. I thought it would dull the pain of…'

This time he didn't try to rush her. He waited until she was ready to start again, and she had never appreciated his calm strength more.

'I knew it wouldn't be exciting, but…' she stopped again and pulled a face as she thought back '…it would definitely be calmer,' she said at last, staring into the distance as she put herself back in the past. 'I pictured myself contented—settled down—an academic's wife even. Perhaps it wasn't the life I'd dreamed about but, then, my fantasies had always let me down.'

'So you slept with him?'

Dante's face was rigid. 'If I'm going to tell you, please let me finish.'

He nodded.

'He wasn't you, but you were no longer part of my life. Someone as different from you as possible seemed the logical answer at the time. It all came to a head one night when he'd taken me out for a meal. I'd had too much to drink. He took me back to his place. I'd seen this coming for a while, which was probably why I drank too much in a failed attempt to numb myself. That's why he's not wholly to blame,' she insisted. 'It's not like I was an innocent, walking into this with my eyes shut. I used him to get over you.'

'Losing a baby would affect you in all sorts of ways,' Dante growled. 'Did he know what you'd been through?'

'Yes, of course. He was my tutor. We were supposed to confide things like that so the tutors could reach out to help us.'

Dante's expression turned grim. 'So you told him everything and he took advantage of your fragile mental state.'

'I allowed him to do it,' she argued stubbornly. 'After losing the baby I felt like a failure. I didn't know if I would ever be anything but—'

'*Deus*, Karina! So, he made it his mission to prove you wrong?' He stared into her face intently. 'How could you put yourself in such a vulnerable position?' And then he slumped back. 'You were already in a vulnerable position,' he groaned softly, answering his own question.

'I had this idea that sex and I were enemies,' she went on over Dante's pain. 'I had to confront my enemy and conquer my fears. If necessary, I was prepared to face the alternative—a life without sex. Lots of people live perfectly happy lives without sex,' she insisted, when Dante stared at her.

'Not in my world,' he ground out.

'Your world's different from most other people's,' she said wryly. 'There's a popular conception that you only have to be young and healthy to be at it like rabbits, but I broke that mould, because I don't like sex.'

Dante's scowl broke into an incredulous laugh. 'And you say that because of your professor?' And then his face darkened again. 'Or are you saying it because of what happened with me?'

She shook her head and thought back. 'He took me to supper and then to bed. I told myself it would be all right. I had put myself on the Pill—belatedly, I know. I just couldn't face another loss. And I had squirrelled away a tube of lubrication, so I can hardly claim to be the innocent party here.' She ignored Dante's look and went on, 'I thought to myself, What can possibly go wrong? He'd do it. I'd be over you, and I would have proved myself normal.'

'So what went wrong with this master plan?' Dante was practically snarling.

'I couldn't do it. When it came to it, I just couldn't do it.' Raising her head, she blazed a look into his eyes. 'Why can't you men accept that some women just don't like sex?'

'Don't speak of me in the same breath as that man,' he warned softly. He let a few moments pass, and then prompted gently, 'Are you ready to tell me the rest?'

She drew a steadying breath. 'I did everything he asked, but then he couldn't do it.' Ignoring Dante's facial expression, she tried to explain. 'He said it was my fault because I wouldn't relax. He said I was too tight for him. I tried to help him but I couldn't, and then he was angry with me, and that's when he fell into a rage—'

'The insect that bit you?' Dante's tone was incredulous.

Lowering the sheet, she took hold of his hand and moved his fingertips slowly over the rest of her scars. 'I ran into a swarm of insects.'

He hissed through his teeth, but let her continue.

'He beat me so much that eventually I fell out of bed, but not before he broke my nose.' Touching it, she huffed a humourless laugh, remembering. 'It wouldn't stop bleeding so I had to go to the emergency room.'

'Did he take you there?'

'No. Of course not. I took myself. He said he was glad to be rid of me, and that I was a pathetic excuse for a woman. Narrow escape, huh?' She tried to smile, but it didn't come off. 'While I was in the emergency room a nurse gave me a full exam. She said it was usual when there was so much bruising. It wasn't just my nose,' she added, quickly staring down to avoid Dante's molten magma stare.

'I told the nurse everything—how he'd tried with his hand, and even with a sex toy he'd bought. It was all a waste of time. I'd…closed up completely. I couldn't understand what had happened to me, until the nurse explained that it's a recognised medical condition. It can be due to physical causes, she told me, though in my case she thought it was more of a psychological reaction to losing the baby and then the violence of that night. She said it wasn't something I could control, and that it would take time and therapy. She fixed me up with a therapist who told me I was lucky I hadn't been raped.' She glanced up. 'That was the end of the therapist. I didn't feel lucky. I felt dirty and ashamed.'

'And now?' Dante's voice was gentle.

'And now I shouldn't be here,' she said, changing her tone to bright and cheerful.

'Because?'

'Because now we both know that there's something wrong with me—and that it could get in the way of our work here.'

'There's nothing wrong with you, Karina.' Dante stated that with such certainty that she didn't even try to resist when he drew her into his arms. 'You've had one trauma after another, and have never given yourself a chance to recover. You're too hard on yourself,' he said, as he pulled back to stare into her face. 'Sometimes it's not possible to bounce back just because we decide it's time. Sometimes we have to ask for help—even you, Karina.' Holding her arms lightly, he brought her in front of him. 'Do you want me to find some professional help for you?'

'No!' She recoiled at the thought.

'You only have to say the word and I'll arrange it with someone who knows what they're doing.'

'Sorry.' Shuddering, she drew in a breath. 'I don't mean to sound ungrateful. It's just that I've tried therapy and I know it doesn't work for me. I honestly think it would set me back.' She said nothing for a long time and then she looked at him. 'Could you help me?'

'I'm going to help you,' Dante confirmed, as if there could be any doubt. 'And I'll do it by starting from scratch.'

'What does that mean?'

'We both know the clock is ticking as far as this event is concerned, so neither of us has the time to concentrate properly on anything else until it's over.'

'What are you saying Dante?'

Easing back, he lifted his shoulders in an easy shrug.

'Whatever happens next will happen naturally, or it won't happen at all.'

Fear of losing him swamped her as he left the bed. She watched him scoop up his jeans and tug them on, feeling she'd already lost him.

'I'm going to leave you to sleep now.' His face was set. His eyes were cool. 'I'll take one of the guest rooms. Tomorrow work on your report. When you're finished, I'll read it. Then we'll have a meeting and decide where to go from here.'

He might even fire her, she thought. Her lips felt wooden as she commented lightly, 'That sounds a bit cold-blooded.'

Dante's stare steadied on her face. 'It is.'

She had to tell herself that what he had suggested made perfect sense, but that didn't stop a chill of apprehension rushing through her. Where would they go from here? Anywhere?

She would concentrate on the event to the exclusion of everything else, she told herself firmly. She would make it the best it could be. She would forget her worthy ideas and go full out for carnival at the Gaucho Cup. She got out of bed, making sure to wrap the sheet tightly around her as she swung her legs over the side. She gasped when Dante snatched the sheet away, leaving her completely naked.

'This is your last day of being a victim, Karina. You're moving forward from now on. You took a wrong turning and that's all.' He shrugged. 'We all make mistakes, as I should know. And here's something else...' He brought his face close. 'You've got me. Understood?'

Did he mean that? Whether he did or not, Dante was right. She would fight back. One day at a time. If she took small steps, instead of trying to leap across chasms, they might even make it together one day, but she couldn't put her life on hold until then. The next time she met Dante it would be on an equal footing, or not at all.

They worked non-stop for the next week, with no time to pause for discussions about anything other than the event, but that didn't mean she stopped feeling. In fact, the cooler Dante became, the more she yearned for his personal attention, but he was clever. He knew her too well. They'd paused for coffee in the yard on her last day on his ranch. Maria had brought it out for them on a tray.

She slanted a glance at him as he issued orders, drank coffee, tapped notes into his phone, and answered questions—anything but mention what had happened between them. Somehow that made his big, powerful body a source of fascination. Had she really shrunk from that? It seemed impossible in theory. Looking at him now, she wanted nothing more than to rub every inch of her against his hard frame. She wanted to taste that bronze skin and, yes, she wanted to remind herself that the straining bulge in his jeans really was that big.

'You look happy,' he commented, sliding her a look.

'Do I?' She glanced around, hoping he hadn't noticed her interest in the manifold attractions of his body. What was wrong with her? She could lust like any normal woman—could yearn for a man's arms around her. She could think the most erotic thoughts, but when it came down to it—

'We'd better get on,' he said, heading off.

Working alongside Dante was a revelation. He was brilliant. Fast thinking and decisive, he was the perfect partner. She had never worked with an associate before. Certainly not one as hot as Dante, she reflected as she walked behind him with the sole purpose of admiring his impressive iron-hard butt. She didn't know anyone else who worked the hours she did, and who barely slept when there was a project to nail down—though the work ethic was a good thing. It kept her sane when frustration of the very real and sexual kind was nagging at her constantly.

If only she could be normal. But if she were there was no time to indulge herself—not at this pace of work. Although, if Dante would care to toss another bucket of icy well water over his head, as he had done this morning in the yard, she was quite happy to take some down time to admire his naked torso—

'Karina?'

'Just thinking through things—making sure I haven't missed anything.' Maintaining an expression of wide-eyed innocence was getting harder by the hour.

'Time to stop thinking and get doing.'

Was he smiling when he turned away? Those black eyes of his were so expressive. And he knew just how to play her. Dante was the master of torment, the maestro of seduction—and he knew it, she thought as he walked away. There was a swagger in his stride and a confidence she suspected had nothing to do with the polo cup.

She braced herself to go and see him before she left the ranch. Half a dozen people were in his study, but he sent them out when she arrived. They both knew she only had a few minutes as a pilot was waiting on the airstrip to take her back to Rio. Final arrangements for the match had reached fever pitch.

'Got everything you need?' he asked.

Not nearly, she thought, taking him in. 'Everything. Thank you.' With his fists braced on the desk as he leaned over it, Dante was like a pent-up volcano just waiting to erupt. It was no surprise to her that he had held the meeting standing up. All that energy…

'I've got something for you.'

'For me?' Her heart stopped.

'A keepsake.' Straightening up, he dug into the back pocket of his jeans and brought out a stone. 'Here—take it.'

She knew what it was and looked at him in surprise. 'Are you sure?' She knew enough about them to know that uncut emeralds were worth a fortune.

'It's just a rough, hard rock.' He said this wryly and she got the message. 'It improves once it's polished up.'

'Some things are fine as they are,' she said, taking it from him.

The corner of his mouth lifted. 'I knew you'd appreciate it.'

She smiled. 'I do. Thank you,' she said quietly, tucking it away in her pocket.

The silence changed and suddenly she felt awkward. Should they kiss on the cheek or shake hands—or neither of the above? She decided to maintain the honoured client routine and shook his hand briefly. That seemed to amuse him, though he overruled the smile and turned his expression to neutral.

She had her hand on the handle on the door when he said, 'You're okay, Karina. You can do this. You don't need anyone now.'

She turned to flash him a quick smile, and tried to pretend that what he'd said was okay. In many ways it was, but it left her uncertain where Dante's feelings for her were concerned.

Maybe that was a good thing?

No, it wasn't.

She drew herself up to tell him, 'I'll be back for the match.'

'Of course.'

'Are you sure I can keep this?' She felt for the stone in her pocket.

'That's what keepsake means,' he said. 'Take it as a reminder of your time here, and all the things we've done together.'

Together. She'd take that word and seal it in her heart.

CHAPTER FIFTEEN

KARINA WAS SO busy when she got back to Rio that her head was spinning. That didn't stop her feelings for Dante keeping her awake at night. They'd put in so much good work on his ranch that everything was falling into place. They worked well together, she reflected as she glanced at his incoming email. She longed to find something personal in them and never did. She still read his new email avidly, as if she were a code-breaker, searching for clues.

After-match party: You know what I expect. Make it the best. Budget no object. D

Elephants? Dancing girls?

She smiled as she shook her head. Dante didn't waste words. Fortunately, she knew what exactly he wanted—carnival, big and brash and bold. And because the honoured client always got what he asked for, carnival was exactly what he was going to get.

The big day of the cup had finally arrived. Dante had hardly had chance to draw breath since Karina had left him at the ranch. His pulse banged as he thought of seeing her again, blood rushing to a part of him that thought about her constantly—inconvenient when he was on a horse. He shifted in the saddle and shouldered his mallet. Nothing had ever mattered to him more than polo. The team had been his family for as long as he could remember. It was his source of warmth and friendship, but now there was another vital element missing in his life—so where the hell was she?

Karina was glad of her VIP pass and doubted she'd make it through the crowds in time without it. Dante's vision was a reality. Carnival in Rio had been transferred to his ranch, and the world was going crazy for it. He was well on track to fulfilling his wish that polo became a popular sport, rather than an elitist game for the fortunate few. She had done everything she could think of to make that possible.

Outside the stadium there were high-quality food outlets, sideshows and a fairground boasting a big wheel, among other rides. There were samba dancers clothed in feathers and sequins performing on the stage, where popular bands were due to take over in the evening. Some of the best musicians in Brazil had offered to give a free concert to raise money for the charities the teams supported, and there was an information pavilion showing all that was best about Brazil.

Everywhere she went people seemed to be dancing and smiling, confirming her impression that the project was a success. Dante was having some quiet time, she'd been told. He'd been away with the team at a secret location, preparing for the match. No one could tell her where he was as the minutes ticked away towards the start, but she had an idea where he might be.

* * *

The ranch house door was on the latch, so she let herself in and quietly closed it behind her. 'Don't stop playing,' she whispered, as he paused in mid-phrase.

Dipping his head in concentration, he started playing again. It drew her across the hall towards him like a magnet. She stopped and smiled. He was such an incongruous sight. Dressed for the match in breeches and a snug-fitting top in his team colours, she doubted there had ever been such a brutal display of muscle and power, and yet the sensitivity in his fingers allowed him to create the most beautiful music. It soothed her like a balm, while he excited her beyond reason.

When the last chord echoed around the hall she stilled, waiting to see what he would do. She had turned away from him to look at a painting as he'd played, and when he walked up behind her she didn't turned around. She remained staring at the same image of the ranch painted just as it had been when he had taken it over. It was a stark reminder of how far he'd come. She had chosen that same image for the back of today's programme, with the most recent image on the front.

'You're back,' he murmured.

Leaning her head towards him, she sought contact, sought warmth, and thrilled all over when his hands gripped her upper arms. She didn't resist him when he lifted them above her head and pinned her against the wall with his weight. Her whole body responded—aching, melting, needing. Arching her back, she thrust her buttocks towards him, responding to those feelings instinctively.

'Keep that thought,' he murmured, dropping a kiss on the back of her neck.

It took a moment of complete stillness before she was capable of turning to watch him stride across the hall in the direction of the front door. Pausing only to grab his helmet and mallet, he headed out for the match.

By the time Dante arrived Team Thunderbolt had assembled. Each man was silent with his own thoughts. This wasn't the time to ask Luc where his sister would be sitting in the crowd. He couldn't believe he'd forgotten to ask Karina where she would be when he had seen her—but he'd had other things on his mind. He had to clear his thoughts now. His colleagues had one thing in mind, and that was obliterating the opposition.

Would he spot Karina in the crowd?

Mounting up, he exchanged a few terse words with his friends. His confidence had never been in doubt where the outcome of this match was concerned, unlike the chance of spotting Karina.

As they rode out to acknowledge the cheers of the crowd, he knew he would entrust his life to the team. They were solid. Their ponies were in top-class condition. They had never been better prepared for a match. He scanned the faceless mass of people. Where was she? He knew she'd be busy with last-minute checks and ground his teeth with frustration as he turned his concentration back to the team.

It was always going to be a close match when the opposing team was captained by the formidable Argentinian Nero Caracas. It all came down to the last chukka. Team Thunderbolt needed one more goal to secure the match...

Nero tried to ride him off, and he was almost unseated, but his pony waited that necessary split second until he was ready, and then she set off again.

He was at full gallop with the goal in his sight when he spotted Karina in the crowd. She wasn't in the stand where he had expected she might sit, but practically on the field, with her body pressed up hard against the barrier. Her face was ashen as she watched Nero chase him down. He could hear the thunder of hooves behind him, but he'd seen Karina, so anything was possible.

And he hadn't just seen her—he'd seen the gold earrings she was wearing—the same gold hoops he'd given to her on her eighteenth birthday.

Raising his mallet, he drove the ball home.

By popular choice, Karina was elected to award the prize. She was waiting at the rostrum for him. 'Congratulations, Dante, and to your team. I always had every confidence in you.'

'As I did in you,' he murmured, as they exchanged chaste kisses of congratulation on each cheek.

'You can let go of my hand now,' she prompted.

As she smiled into his eyes he realised that his teammates were backed up behind him, with the opposing team members also waiting to receive their medals. He smiled and stepped back.

When all the presentations had been made, he lifted the trophy in the air to rapturous cheers from the crowd, but for once in his life all he could think about was being somewhere else—preferably in a nice firm bed with Karina.

Karina was very relieved that Thunderbolt had won, but she was even more relieved that Dante was safe. She felt alert and alive, excited and light-headed as Dante looked at her over the heads of his teammates. They were separated by convention and not much more. They had to see the presentation ceremony through to the end, but the tension between them was like a high wire stretched taut.

She told herself to be patient. It would be some time before they could be alone.

At last the podium cleared and Dante left with the other players to check on the horses. She found him in the stables, where he was rewarding each animal in turn with affection and treats. The ponies' ears were pricked, and they seemed as proud as Dante was of their victory. Somewhere in the distance she could hear a band starting up. They were alone. Everyone else had left to go to the party, which would be an all-nighter.

'Hey…congratulations,' she said, leaning over the half-door of the stall.

'To you too,' Dante said, without looking up as he checked this pony's legs. 'You made one hell of an event here today, Karina.'

'I didn't do it on my own.'

Dante hummed.

For a moment she couldn't think straight. Just looking at him was enough, though his strength went a lot further than power and muscle. He was a good man. He was an exciting man. He was a gaucho. He was a working man, who was entirely the opposite from the glamorous playboy the press liked to portray.

'You wore my earrings,' he said, viewing her through narrowed eyes as he straightened up.

'For you… For good luck.'

Leaving the stall, he bolted the door and turned to face her.

'And I brought you this.' She tossed the stone he'd

given her and with whip-fast reflexes Dante caught it in his fist as it spun through the air.

'Now what?' he murmured, staring at her darkly as he tightened his big hand around it.

'Now you kiss me.'

They came together like a force of nature. This was where she wanted to be. She belonged in Dante's arms. He laughed deep down in his chest, as if the same feeling had hit him in the same moment, and then he backed her steadily towards a bed of hay.

'At last,' he ground out. 'Though this wasn't quite the setting I had in mind.'

'Where better than here?' she argued, breathlessly stripping off his clothes.

It was like a race to remove the last barrier between them, and Dante devoured her mouth as he lowered her onto the hay. There was no need to say anything. A look conveyed all they needed to know. This was the man she knew and remembered. This was her friend, the man she had always trusted, always loved. This was redemption. This was the end of a very long journey. This was coming home. Stroking her hair, Dante brought her close to drop a kiss on her collarbone and then her neck. He laughed softly when she whimpered with pleasure.

Karina was the only woman who could tame him. She was his equal in every way. She was the only woman he could think of spending his life with. There was only one question remaining now. 'I love you,' he whispered.

She stared into his eyes as if she needed to be absolutely sure, but then she smiled. 'I love you too.'

He brought her into his arms to promise her that he would give her babies, and instead of flinching from him in doubt and fear she looked into his eyes with trust and laughter. 'Right now?' she asked him, smiling into his eyes.

'Why not now? Whatever fate and Dante Baracca dictates,' he teased her gently, and then, kissing her, he soothed her as he led her at his pace into an erotic world.

He was determined that everything would be perfect for Karina. She deserved nothing less. She'd known violence and grief, and had no reason to trust a man. It was up to him to prove that he was different. There was still a glimmer of fear in her eyes. Until she tried it, she didn't know how it would work out. He understood her concerns, and was going to prove that she was normal in every way. Even now, when passion had never run higher between them, he was going to give her all the time she needed to discover that he was right. She tensed a little when he moved over her, and again when his hand found her. She was ready in every sense, and that was all he needed to know.

She flinched when Dante eased her legs over his shoulders. She felt so exposed, so vulnerable, and was worried that she might still disappoint him, but he was endlessly patient, and so sexy that she couldn't overlook the fact that her body was entirely on his side. Positioning her, he cupped her buttocks and when he dipped his head it was to give her pleasure on a scale that didn't allow for rational thought. She could only feel—wave after wave of incredible sensation.

Lifting his head, he said wryly, 'Why are you waiting?'

'I've got no idea,' she admitted, realising she was clutching handfuls of hay in her fists, as if that could stop her falling off the edge.

'Then don't,' he advised.

Dante didn't give her a chance to argue, and she cried out with shock at the intensity of feeling. He had to hold her firmly. She was wild with pleasure. She was exultant. She was free. She was also breathless and moaning out her approval of everything he did, as Dante made sure she enjoyed every last second of release. But it was more than that, she reasoned as he brushed kisses over her face and neck to soothe her down. They were well on the way to rebuilding everything they'd lost.

She made no pretence of holding back a second time. Dante had taught her something else about her body today. The deeper he led her into his sensual world, the more she wanted him, and the more sensitive she became. Lowering her legs from his shoulders, he drew her into his arms and lay with her in silence for a while, but the instant his hand found her, she closed her thighs around it to increase the pressure and the pleasure, as she worked with him, moving rhythmically and steadily towards her goal.

She'd almost reached it when Dante slid one lean finger deep inside her. Her body was so slick and welcoming there was no tension, no pain, only pleasure. She trusted him completely. He knew how far to go, and he didn't try to rush her or move too fast. Far from shrinking from him, she rolled her hips to catch more pleasure, working her tender bud against the heel of his hand. Soon the pressure began building again, and almost immediately she found herself teetering on the edge.

He'd said don't wait...

Dante held her as she fell and shrieked his name. The pleasure was indescribable and now she realised that it had increased with his penetration. She worked her body hard against his hand as the violent pleasure waves went on and on, and when he suggested more, she warned him not to stop.

'You're smiling?' he growled, bringing her beneath him.

'Because I can do this.'

'Of course you can do this.' Shaking his head with amused exasperation, he dropped kisses on her swollen mouth and brought a second finger into play, and soon even that wasn't enough for her, and reaching down she found him.

'Don't,' he warned.

'Are you saying you'd lose control?'

'I'm saying that holding back is torture enough already.'

He groaned as she caressed him. She loved the feel of him beneath her hands, the heightened sense of anticipation that a promise of commitment was waiting to be sealed between them.

'You have the perfect body,' Dante murmured, working some magic of his own. 'If I had my way you'd never get dressed.'

'If you had your way, nothing would ever get done.'

'You'd get done,' he whispered.

Brushing back her hair, he stared into her face. 'I love you more than life itself, Karina. I've always loved you. You were mine from the first moment I saw you.'

'Do you mean the day you sauntered into my father's stables while I was sitting on a hay bale, eating my lunch?'

'Why?'

'The lunch you stole from me and fed to the dogs?'

Dante eased his powerful shoulders in a lazy shrug. 'What clearer sign can a boy give a girl that he's interested?'

She moved over him to lean on his chest. 'You owe me lunch.'

He laughed. 'I'll have to do something about that. Lunch in kind?'

'I am now officially insatiable,' she agreed.

'And perfect.'

'And I love you.'

'I know you do,' Dante agreed with a wicked smile.

'You're such an arrogant…'

'Barbarian?' he suggested. Smiling seductively, she moved down the hay. She tasted him and then drew him deep into her mouth.

'What did I warn you about torturing me?' he demanded in a strangled tone.

'I just like to hear you gasp,' she admitted huskily as Dante drew her up to him. Turning her beneath him, he repeated the stroking motion until it was her turn to beg. 'Please…'

'Your wish is my command,' he murmured, and slowly sinking deep he filled her completely. Pausing until she had totally relaxed and temporarily stopped gasping with pleasure, he stared into her eyes and began to move. He only managed a few firm thrusts before she fell helpless and screaming into a deep black pit of ecstasy. And when he started moving once more, rhythmically and firmly, she fell a second time, even harder than the first.

'More?' he suggested wryly when she quieted.

'If you ever stop…'

'I've no intention of stopping, but I do think we should take this to the ranch house so there are no interruptions in the morning.'

With that kind of promise she made no complaint.

Withdrawing slowly and carefully, Dante helped her

to her feet, and wordlessly they grabbed their clothes and pulled them on, then he grabbed her hand and walked with her out of the stable block. By the time they exited they were running. They ran across the yard, barged into the house, slammed the door behind them and raced up the stairs. They crashed into his bedroom and fell on the bed, where they ripped off each other's clothes in a frenzy of hunger and need. There was no foreplay this time, none necessary. Dante spun her beneath him and entered her in one deep, firm stroke.

They were wild with excitement, and breathless with the energy required to make love furiously and hard. All her fears had left her and had been replaced with a desire to be one with Dante. And once definitely wasn't enough—not for either of them. They had to endorse the mating of their souls, their trust in each other, and their love, over and over again. And still he left her whimpering with urgent need.

'More,' she whispered, stroking his powerful chest.

'Oh, must I?' Dante teased her, sinking deep with an exquisite lack of haste.

Rotating his hips to a lazy rhythm, he kept on until she couldn't control herself, and moving convulsively, she fell into yet another delicious climax. Her cries rang out as her body bucked uncontrollably. She was glad of his big hands on her buttocks, holding her firmly, guiding her movements, ensuring that she benefited from every single pleasure pulse until they faded.

'Good?' he murmured, when she quietened.

'But not good for you—not fair,' she protested.

She was greedy for her next release and, reading her, Dante smiled. Bracing himself on his forearms, he stared down into her face. 'I'd say you were being more than good to me.' And to prove it, he thrust deep.

Holding him with her inner muscles, she moved with him, and this time when she fell he fell too, finally claiming his own savage release, and when they finally fell back exhausted, she knew the ghosts of the past had been banished for good, and she drifted off into a contented slumber. And when she woke they were still entwined in each other's arms.

'Do you think there's the smallest chance we'll ever get enough of each other?' she asked, her lips touching his as she murmured this.

'Hopefully not,' Dante said, smiling, 'though I think I should put that to the test on a regular basis, don't you?'

'Why not now?' she agreed, as he moved behind her.

Thrusting his hand into the small of her back he lifted her buttocks, exposing her even more to him. Seconds later he was sheathed to the hilt. Arching her back, she pressed back hard against him. 'You're right,' she managed breathlessly before giving herself over completely to pleasure. 'Who could ever get enough of this?'

It was dark and the night was full of stars and romance by the time they left the ranch house. Parties for all age groups were in full swing and music rose around them on every side. Samba rhythms added to the heat of the night as they walked together arm in arm. It was only when they smelled the scent of food grilling on countless barbeques that they realised they couldn't remember the last time they'd had something to eat. They stopped to grab some sticky ribs, and that was where Luc found them.

'There you are!' he exclaimed. 'Where on earth have you been?'

Karina was careful to keep her innocent face on. She

adored her brother, but once again Luc had proved that when it came to his sister he was incapable of registering the possibility of romance.

'We've been checking the horses,' Dante said, carefully not looking at Karina. 'I didn't realise you needed us.'

'Of course you're needed,' Luc said, as he swung an arm around Dante's shoulder. 'In case you've forgotten, you scored the winning goal, and my sister organised the event. There's a huge crowd waiting to thank you.'

Karina glanced at Dante and laughed. As she finger-combed her hair, she realised there was still some hay sticking in it, and her hands were covered with sticky sauce. Luc still didn't have a clue.

'Here,' he said, whipping off his bandana. 'Wipe your hands. And for goodness' sake, do something about your hair—' He stopped suddenly, and stared at her intently. 'Oh,' he said, and then he spun on his heel.

Fireworks lit up the sky as they mounted the stage. The applause was deafening, and in spite of his recent epiphany Luc had recovered sufficiently to give them both a more than generous introduction. 'For my team-mate and friend, Dante Baracca…' Covering the mike with his hand, Luc murmured to Dante, 'You'd better do the honourable thing or I'll rip your head off.' Turning, he smiled for the benefit of the crowd.

'Trust me. I intend to,' Dante growled, as he brought Karina close.

'And for my sister, who arranged this whole event,' Luc continued, once the cheers had died down, 'I couldn't be happier for you both,' he admitted gruffly, as glittering confetti cascaded down from the nets suspended about their heads and the crowd went wild.

'Nothing—not even this trophy—means as much to me as you do,' Dante told Karina, as they stood together to take the applause. And then he provided them all with the surprise of the day. Handing the trophy to Luc, he got down on one knee. To the delight of the crowd, he asked, 'Could you marry a barbarian?'

'Now I've tamed him?' She pretended to think about it as the crowd waited in a breathless hush. 'Yes,' she said softly, 'I can definitely marry the man I love.' And then she covered the mike with her hand. 'I always knew barbarians could be romantic, but aren't you afraid of spoiling your image?'

She laughed as Dante sprang up.

'I don't care about my image,' he said, as he swung her into his arms and carried her away into the night.

CHAPTER SIXTEEN

HOW THINGS HAD CHANGED, Karina mused as she hosted the two men she loved best in the world in her new and much larger office. The Gaucho Cup held on Dante's *fazenda* had been such a success that the team had voted for it to be held each year at Fazenda Baracca, with Karina arranging the event.

'You can't get out of it now that you and Dante are to be married,' her brother remarked as he stared with pride at the gleaming replica trophy that had barely left his hands since Karina had awarded it to him. The team had decided the original cup should stay with one man, and that man was Dante.

'Are you threatening my fiancée?' Dante growled, as the two men locked stares.

'Yeah,' Luc agreed happily. 'I can't think of two people who deserve each other more.'

'So this was all your idea?' Karina smiled at her brother, who refused to meet her eyes, making her instantly suspicious that he'd set her up—though, on this one occasion, she was prepared to forgive him as she stared at Dante and then at the beautiful emerald ring he'd given her—the same rough stone, her keepsake, now polished to its full eye-catching glory.

'I always knew you'd make a good team,' Luc murmured distractedly, as he paced the room to admire the trophy, which he had placed temporarily on her desk, from several different angles.

'Is that why you volunteered me for the job?'

'Could be,' Luc admitted, 'though I got some persuasion from a certain direction.' He glanced at Dante.

'That's enough, Luc,' Dante warned, as he gathered Karina into his arms. 'And now you'll have to excuse us as Karina and I have another appointment…' Walking to the door, he held it open. 'See you at the engagement party tonight.'

'I'll be there,' Luc promised, fielding Karina's accusatory look with an unapologetic grin. 'I wouldn't miss it for the world,' he assured them, flashing Dante an amused glance as he snatched up his precious trophy.

'We've got another appointment?' Karina queried once the door had closed behind her brother.

'You're a very busy woman,' Dante murmured, as he turned the key in the lock.

'Dante, we can't.'

'Who makes the rules around here?'

'Well, I do, but…'

Dante raised a brow and then raised her hands above her head as he pressed her back against the wall.

'Keep that thought?' she suggested, her pulse shooting up as Dante stared into her eyes.

'Not for long,' he assured her. Lifting her skirt, he dispensed with her underwear and let it drift to the floor.

'Please,' she gasped, all out of reasons why they shouldn't as she locked her legs around his waist.

'It would be my absolute pleasure,' Dante assured her, sinking to the hilt with his first firm thrust.

Losing control almost immediately, she had to bury her face in his shoulder to muffle her cries of pleasure as he rammed her repeatedly against the wall.

'Again?' he suggested dryly, when she quieted, knowing what her answer would be.

'Do you need to ask?'

He chuckled softy as he tightened his hold on her buttocks. 'I have to take advantage of you while I can,' he murmured against her mouth.

Dante was referring to her workload, which had increased considerably since the Gaucho Cup. News of her success had spread rapidly, and her diary was crammed to the point where Dante had asked her in all seriousness if she would have time to get married. 'On the hoof,' she had told him dryly. 'In between arranging the sheikh's wedding, and the naming of the Greek's ship.'

Dante, of course, came up with the perfect solution. They'd get engaged on one day and married the next, and then spend the rest of their life enjoying a series of honeymoons.

'You are a very bad man,' she told him much, *much* later when they were on their way out of the building.

'What are elevators for?' he demanded, when she made a half-hearted attempt to stop him with her hands pressed flat against his chest.

'They're for going up and down,' she said, frowning at his question.

'Exactly my point,' he agreed.

Their engagement party was being held at a café in the projects, and Karina's face was wreathed in smiles when she saw how many people had turned out to wish them well. Several samba bands had come along and the drums were thundering as they walked into the square. Everyone was in their best costume, with feathers in rainbow hues and enough sequins to sink a small ship. Swinging her into his arms, Dante held her close as they moved to the samba rhythms. 'They love you almost as much as I do,' he said, dropping kisses on her neck.

'I'm just so glad everyone can celebrate with us, but you did say it would just be a few of friends, along with Jada, the girl I sponsor, and her mother, and some people from the café.'

'Don't you prefer this?'

'You know I do, but I can't believe how many people are here.'

'What?' Dante asked with concern when her expression changed to a frown.

'Do you think that elevator has been reported out of order?'

'Let Luc worry about that,' Dante soothed. 'This is your night off, remember?'

He laughed as she pulled a face and the next moment they were in the thick of it, with everyone surrounding them. Dante's teammates and their wives were waiting for them too, but it was more like a gathering of a happy clan than a group of rampaging barbarians.

Which was the truth of the matter after all, and just the way it should be, Karina reflected happily as Dante led her into the café, with all their guests crowding in behind them. What use was a rampaging barbarian without a strong woman to channel all that energy?

She wouldn't change Dante in any way. They had both been isolated and mistrustful. Dante because of a father who had derided everything he'd done, while she had hidden from the world after losing the baby until it had become a habit she couldn't break. But they were stronger together than they had ever been apart. She'd heard that the professor who had abused her had recently lost his job, and was being held by the police for attacking several other women.

When she had asked Dante how his cruelty had first come to light, all she got was a shrug, but not before she'd seen the flash of warrior fire in his eyes.

'Happy?' he murmured, pulling her into his hard body.

'As I've ever been,' she said honestly.

'Well, that's lucky, because you, soon-to-be Senhora Baracca, are vital to my existence.'

'As you are to mine,' she said. 'What?' she asked, instantly suspicious, when she saw a particular look flash in Dante's eyes.

His lips pressed down as he gave her a wicked look. 'No one will notice if we slip away.'

'Of course they will—it's our engagement party.'

'We'll say we're making arrangements for the wedding.'

'But our wedding's tomorrow,' she said, as he guided her through the crowd. 'And all the arrangements have been made. I made them myself, so I should know.'

'Karina,' Dante murmured, as he pulled her into the shadows. 'There's no law against rehearsing for our wedding night, is there?'

'If there were such a law, you'd surely break it.'

'That's my duty as a barbarian,' Dante insisted, as he steered her ahead of him.

'So you just want me for sex?'

'I definitely want you for sex. And for the baby we're going to make. I can't do it without you,' he pointed out.

'How have we managed to leave the party without anyone noticing?' she marvelled.

'A tribute to your good planning,' Dante insisted, as he edged her deeper into the shadows. 'Everyone is enjoying themselves so much they haven't noticed that the guests of honour have left.' Kissing her, he frowned as he rested his hand on her stomach. 'And I really do need to make a start on your most important project for this year.'

'A start?' she queried. 'I thought we'd already done that several times over.'

'There's nothing wrong with perfecting our technique.'

'Dante…'

Suddenly scared at the thought of a baby, she clung to him, but Dante's confidence remained rock solid. 'I'll be with you every step of the way,' he said quietly and intently. 'And you're strong, Karina, never forget that.'

'*We're* strong,' she agreed.

'Together we're stronger,' Dante confirmed. Dragging her against his hot, hard body, his lips tugged in the familiar smile that could always melt her, as her barbarian lover kissed the woman he adored.

EPILOGUE

CHRISTMAS WAS ALWAYS a special time of year, but this year there was an extra miracle in the Baracca household as Dante showed off their son to the world. Reporters had come from every part of the globe to witness the transformation of yet another rampaging barbarian into a happily married family man.

'He looks just like me,' Dante proudly told the waiting press.

'Like a barbarian?' Karina murmured beneath her breath. 'He's far more beautiful than that.'

'At the moment,' Dante agreed with a frown as he studied his son's face. 'But he'll no doubt grow rugged and tough like his father in time.'

'I don't care what he grows into, so long as he's happy,' Karina argued, once they were alone.

'You know I feel the same,' Dante reassured her. They had returned to the fabulous penthouse apartment in Rio that Dante had bought for his wife as a wedding present.

'But I bet you've already picked out his first pony,' Karina guessed.

'Of course I have,' Dante said, as if anything else were unthinkable. 'My son will be the most famous polo player in the world.'

'Of course he will.' Karina smiled at her own, personal barbarian. 'And I'm glad we're both thinking along the same lines because, as it happens, I've already picked out his wife.'

'You have?' Dante's gaze turned suddenly fierce as it clashed with hers.

'No, of course I haven't,' she said with a groan of amusement. 'We've both agreed that our children will choose their own paths through life. Our son may not even like horses.'

'Unthinkable!' Dante exclaimed, dismissing this preposterous idea immediately.

'Whatever he decides to do, I know we'll back him to the hilt.'

Dante grunted and frowned, but as he passed his infant son over to the woman he loved more than anything else in the world, he knew Karina was right. Their children would have two loving parents to encourage them in everything they did.

'Do you think that having a wife and an infant son with reflect badly on the image of the team?' Karina asked later, when they were standing on their balcony in Rio, watching the fireworks go off to herald the advent of Christmas Day.

'It changes nothing about the team,' Dante assured her. 'If anything, it adds a new dimension, a new mystique.'

'Giving hope to women everywhere that a rampaging barbarian can be tamed?' she suggested wryly.

'With the right woman—someone strong and stubborn like you,' Dante agreed.

'I must be a glutton for punishment,' she said, snuggling close.

'Talking of which,' Dante murmured, 'you did say a glutton for pleasure?'

'That too,' Karina admitted wryly as she steered Dante back into the bedroom.

* * * * *

Meet the rest of the Thunderbolt polo team in the
HOT BRAZILIAN NIGHTS! *series:*

CHRISTMAS NIGHTS WITH THE POLO PLAYER
IN THE BRAZILIAN'S DEBT
AT THE BRAZILIAN'S COMMAND
BRAZILIAN'S NINE MONTHS' NOTICE

Available now!

Maisey Yates

Christmas at The Chatsfield

LUCY KENNEWICK HATED CHRISTMAS. She had for the past five years. Every single year she had spent in her husband's—soon-to-be ex-husband's—sterile mansion, void of boughs of holly, mistletoe or anything resembling a reindeer, had been bleak and soulless like the man himself.

Before her marriage to Nico she had quite liked Christmas in New York. From the beautiful department-store window displays to the glittering tree in Rockefeller Center. But after that all of the festive cheer outside had only been a reminder of the starkness inside her life.

She lifted the red skirt of her gown as she walked up the steps that led to the front entrance to the grand ballroom of the Chatsfield. This would be her first Christmas party without him since they were married, and she was determined to enjoy herself.

They had both been invited. Because when the invitations had been sent out their marriage had still been seamless, as far as the public eye was concerned.

Though, the iconic marriage of Lucy Kennewick and Nico Katsaros had never been all that it had appeared.

A marriage to shore up her failing company. A marriage of convenience.

Though, a *real* marriage. In spite of the fact they had never shared a room, never shared their personal space, they had most certainly shared a bed.

As Lucy walked into the ballroom she unbuttoned her long black coat, handing it to the man waiting to check it. As she did she became suddenly conscious of her hands, of the fact that her left hand was bare. That her ring was gone.

That her marriage was over.

She should be happy. The day after Christmas everything would be finalized, and her life would go back to normal. Her marriage to Nico would be nothing more than a blip on the radar. A starter marriage. Who in the city didn't have one of those?

She made her way deeper into the room, feeling suddenly very conscious in the bright red silk gown amid the sea of chic New York City black. The annual Christmas ball was always a can't-miss event, but since the takeover of the new CEO, interest had been heightened. So many of the people here were in attendance because they were searching for something. For a sign of weakness, for a way to ally with Spencer Chatsfield. And Lucy?

Lucy simply wanted to take this chance to start over.

But she had one thing in common with the rest of the guests. She was wearing a mask over her eyes, offering the thinnest veil of anonymity. Making her feel as though she was watching all of those around her, while keeping herself hidden from them.

Suddenly she felt a prickling sensation on the back of her neck and she lifted her head, looking into a mirror that was mounted on the wall in front of her. She could see herself, dark hair styled into loose waves, the golden mask fitted to her face, red lips, painted to match the crimson gown that formed to her slight curves, parted as if in shock.

And then she saw what had caused the prickling sensation. She had been wrong. She had been seen. Someone else was watching her. In the reflection of the mirror, her eyes connected to those of the man behind her. He was wearing a black mask, his flawless body outlined to perfection in the custom-made suit he was wearing.

Those dark eyes saw through her mask. And she saw through his.

Nico Katsaros. Her first husband. Her first lover, but never her first love. Because he didn't believe in it. And she didn't want it.

The ghost of Christmas past had come to haunt her indeed.

His wife was here. And she had the nerve to look like every Christmas present he'd been denied as a child.

Then, as now, seeing the brightly wrapped gift, all he wanted to do was to tear back the paper and reveal the treasure beneath. Then, as now, he was forbidden from doing so.

The child of a maid living in a palatial estate, he had witnessed grandeur on a massive scale from a very early age. Witnessed it, but not been allowed to partake of it.

He hated being denied. Then and now.

She was beautiful, Lucy was. She always had been. And when she had proposed a marriage of convenience between the two of them to help improve his playboy image, and to add her ailing company to his list of assets, he had been more than willing. A wife was the next logical acquisition for him, and one as beautiful as Lucy could never be a hardship.

Tonight she had outdone herself. The gown was beautiful, but he was fixated on what the pale skin beneath it looked like. He knew. He knew intimately. The silky texture, every delicate curve of her body.

He and Lucy had always been able to talk business, and they had always been able to make love.

It was everything else they found challenging.

Sex had never been an issue. He had wondered at first, because when he'd met Lucy she had seemed quite severe. All business. And yet, the way her suits had been tailored to her exquisite body had given him a hint that she was a woman who knew her appeal and also knew how to use it.

During their very short engagement they had discovered that the business arrangement was not the only perk of their union. Their attraction had been combustible from the beginning. Though, she had made him wait for their wedding night, and he had been rewarded spectacularly with her innocence and the most explosive encounter of his life.

Every encounter thereafter had only been better. And for five years, even as he felt the gulf widen between them their physical intimacy had only grown more intense.

Until she had told him she was leaving. Until she had told him it was over.

After that, all of the lust he had felt had turned into burning, brilliant hatred. As white-hot as any passion that had ever passed between them before.

Though, seeing her now, he knew that not all of the lust between them had been eradicated.

Crystal blue eyes met his in the reflection of the mirror and he began to walk toward her. The same eyes widened in horror, her lush red lips pressing into a firm line. She did not want him to talk to her. All the more reason to approach.

"Merry Christmas, *agape mou*."

Those words. Oh, dear God, those words. They had always ignited a fire in her stomach. And parts lower.

"It isn't Christmas yet, Nico." She swallowed hard, bracing herself to turn and face him, to deal with the man in the flesh rather than as a ghost reflected before her. "There are still a few hours left."

She turned, and realized too late that there was no bracing herself for impact when it came to him. Her only consolation was that the mask blunted some of his masculine beauty, the black leather concealing his strong brow and his cheekbones. But it did nothing to reduce the intensity of his dark gaze. And it certainly didn't stop her stomach from tightening painfully. Didn't stop her body from responding.

Five years she had shared his bed and nothing had taken the edge off of her desire for him.

Not even when she had grown bitter, broken over the distance that remained between them.

No matter how many times she kissed him, no matter how many times she let him inside her body, she never felt closer to him. They had sex, but they did not have intimacy. And there came a point where she could no longer bear it.

"You wouldn't know it. Based on the department-store displays, one would assume Christmas began in October."

"And yet, I would venture to say that based on our

own work schedules you wouldn't know it was Christmas at all."

"What are you doing with your time these days, Lucy?"

Since you no longer have your company. The rest of the sentence remained unspoken.

She had lost Kennewick Manufacturing when she had chosen to divorce Nico. But among the many things she had learned about herself over the past few years was the fact that she now knew business couldn't fill every void. She needed more. And in order to have more, she had to escape her marriage.

"Right now? Volunteer work. I haven't decided anything about my future yet. It may surprise you to know that I'm eminently employable."

He chuckled, the dark sound rolling over her like a hit of good alcohol, warming her, making her light-headed. "That doesn't surprise me at all. You have a keen business mind, even if you are a faithless wife."

"I was never once unfaithful to you, Nico."

"Betraying your marriage vows by seeking divorce is not unfaithful?"

Lucy gritted her teeth. "Divorce is legal. I was your wife, not your prisoner."

"As the holidays have slowed things up you are still my wife."

She looked down, swallowing, or rather, trying to. Her throat was so dry she felt as though she had been snacking on cotton balls. "Yes, well, another reason to dislike this time of year."

"Perhaps you should speak to our host Spencer Chatsfield about getting a job? I'm sure the new CEO of the Chatsfield Empire would be delighted to have you. The rumor is that he is out to acquire the Harrington chain of hotels as well, so I imagine there will be more job opportunities open for those who are already in house. One would think those at the Harrington will be out of luck."

"Why would you think I'd have any interest in that?"

"Because you have a thing for powerful men, and Spencer Chatsfield is most certainly that."

Rage zipped down her spine. "Is that what you think of me? That the only way I could possibly get ahead is to use a man?"

"Your track record would suggest that as a possibility," he said, his voice hard. "However, you are wrong. It is not what I think of you. Because I do not think of you at all."

The lie burned his tongue. He thought of her. He thought of her every night as he tried to sleep. He'd thought of her when he tried to pick up a woman in a club only a few nights ago. He thought of nothing but Lucy. His body wanted no woman but Lucy.

Inconvenient, since he despised Lucy.

Their life had been comfortable, until she had left. Nothing had changed. He had not changed.

She had changed.

She had left him. And he was not done with her.

Standing there right now, looking at her in that dress, his fingers itching to tear it from her body, he *knew* he was not done with her.

The mask did nothing to dull her beauty. If anything, it added mystery.

Mystery. That was intriguing, considering the fact she had been in his bed for five years, considerably longer than any other woman in his life ever had been. And he had been faithful to her. He had not been certain he could manage that when they'd first married. But it had been easy. He'd never wanted anyone else.

Which was the issue now, considering she was no longer his wife, or rather, wouldn't be on the day after Christmas.

But he had let her walk out. He had let her do so without a fight.

He had let her get away too easy. Perhaps being married to her had made him soft. In the past no one would have dared to find Nico Katsaros in that way.

He had allowed Lucy to make him forget who he was.

And it was time that both she, and he, remembered.

"Do you know, as we have been standing here talking I find I'm remembering something," he said.

"What?" she asked.

"I am very angry with you."

"You are angry with me?" Her blue eyes flashed with rage. "You think you have the right to be angry with me?"

"Oh yes, I have every right. You made vows to me, *agape*. And you have broken them."

"Why should you care? It isn't as though you love me."

Her words hung between them, resting just below the soft strains of Christmas music that were drifting through the air.

"I do not have to love you to want you," he said.

"It would be nice if you didn't hate me."

"The sex was very hot between us when our feelings were much more bland. Imagine how good it could be now."

Her pale cheeks flushed red. "That's neither here nor there, as having sex with the man you are divorcing is hardly advisable."

"But you are wearing a mask. As am I. We could be anyone."

"But we are not," she said, her breasts rising on a sharp breath.

"So serious, Lucy," he said. "Always. Much too serious."

"Life is serious. You have never seemed to take it that way."

"Obviously you don't know me very well, Lucy."

Furious blue eyes met his. "Whose fault is that?"

"It doesn't matter. Not if we are strangers."

He let the words simmer there for a moment.

The fire in her eyes chilled, crystallized. "What exactly are you proposing?"

"That we leave the past here. And go upstairs and have one last night together. One last Christmas. You look every inch like a present just for me, and I find I cannot wait to unwrap you."

Lucy could only stare at her husband, stunned.

Nico was holding out forbidden fruit, and she desperately wanted to grab hold of it. To do more than simply take a bite. To seize it, to savor it.

But even as she battled her desire to speak the *yes* that hovered on her lips, her insides curled in on themselves, retreating as though they'd been touched by fire.

Because she remembered why she'd asked for the divorce in the first place. Because she remembered that sex—no matter how good—couldn't replace real, emotional intimacy. That it wouldn't fill the emptiness in her, or fix the loneliness that always hit her with the force of a hurricane after they finished making love and Nico went back to his own bedroom.

Which meant that no matter how intensely her body burned, she could not submit herself to that kind of pain. Not again.

"This *present* is no longer for you."

His dark eyes burned into hers. "Is that so? Is someone else going to open you up this year, *agape*?"

"Perhaps," she lied.

"Then you must point him out to me," Nico said, his tone hard.

"For what purpose?"

"So that I can kill him."

A strange little zip of pleasure wound its way through her body. Nico was passionate about business, he was passionate in the bedroom, but in his verbal exchanges with her he had never been anything but measured, calm. Disinterested almost. He had certainly never expressed jealousy. And that was what this was, jealousy. Her soon-to-be ex-husband was jealous. Of a fictional man who didn't exist anywhere outside of a tiny little implied falsehood.

"You're *not* going to kill my lover," she said, unable to resist pushing him a little bit further.

"You think not? But then you must ask yourself, Lucy, if you ever knew me."

"If I didn't know you, whose fault was it? Mine or yours, Nico?"

"Perhaps it is both of ours."

She sucked in a sharp breath. "Do you think so? I never kept anything from you."

He reached out, taking hold of her chin to study her face, forcing her eyes to meet his. "Did you not?" His gaze was intense, focused. He slid his thumb along her bottom lip, sending sparks of pleasure along her spine. "I very much believe that you kept secrets from me."

Every guilty word she had left unspoken between them built up inside her chest. "I can't fathom you would have ever cared to hear my secrets."

"So instead you will tell them to another man?"

"What will I get in return if I tell them to you?"

"Pleasure. Have I ever denied you pleasure?"

"No." She blinked hard. "But in the end it wasn't enough."

"For a marriage, perhaps. But for a night?"

She cleared her throat. "Even if I did intend to sleep with another man, you would try to seduce me away from him?"

"If in fact you do intend to sleep with another man tonight, then I am certainly angry with you. But not angry enough to cut off my nose to spite my face, so to speak. And anyway, I would rather have you in my bed than know you were in bed with someone else."

"And what about you? Going back to the legions of women you used to have before you married me?"

"There has been no one else. I want no one else," he said, his voice rough.

"Really?" His words soothed the wound she hadn't been aware was there.

"But it was not the same for you?"

"Of course there is no one else. There was no one before you. Why would I find another lover so quickly after you?"

A slow, satisfied smile spread over his features. And she knew she had made a mistake. Knew that she had forgotten she was talking to a predator. One who saw her as prey.

"Perhaps I should not be so gratified to hear this, but I am."

"That does not mean I'm going to sleep with you."

"All right," he said, his tone measured, calm. She wasn't fooled. "But if you will not sleep with me, perhaps you would consider dancing with me?"

Nico's heart was pounding in his head, the metallic tang of anger only just now receding from his tongue. It had been a lie, and he was grateful for it. She was still his wife, after all, even if it was for only one more day.

After that, once she was no longer his, she could have whomever she wanted. But until then, she belonged to him. If she was spending the night in anyone's bed in these last remaining hours of their marriage, it would be his.

"Dance with me," he repeated.

"Just a dance?"

"If you wish."

He extended his hand, his chest tightening as he evaluated the expression on her face, partially concealed by the golden mask. There was fear in her eyes, trepidation. He had not seen her look at him that way since their wedding night. When she had been a virgin. When she had been filled with uncertainty as to what would pass between them. He had taught her, and quickly, that there was nothing to fear from him, not the marriage bed. And while they had never trusted each other with everything, they had trusted each other physically. He could see that he had lost that during their six months of separation.

But then, she intended to separate from him forever, so perhaps that should not come as a surprise.

"One dance," he said, unable to remain patient. Unable to wait for her to make the next move.

"One." She curled her delicate fingers around his and he fought the urge to cling to her tightly, to tug her against his chest and kiss her now, to prove to her that whatever she believed, whatever she pretended, whatever those signed divorce papers waiting to be filed said, her body still belonged to him.

He resisted, but only just, playing the part of gentleman as he led her out to the dance floor. Everything in him longed to pull her tight against him, and yet he managed to draw her into a respectful closed hold.

Oh yes, he was very much playing the part of the gentleman he'd never been.

The better to lure you into bed, my dear.

She looked up at him, blue eyes wide, as though she had heard the thought. He said nothing, only raising an eyebrow in response.

He was unbearably conscious of the feel of her skin beneath his. And of the fact her hand seemed different somehow.

Her ring. Her ring was gone.

"You have taken off my ring?" he asked.

"Yes. We're divorcing." She looked down and he knew then she'd caught sight of the gold band he still wore on his left hand. "You still wear yours?"

"I was not the one who asked for a divorce," he said, his tone closing the subject neatly.

He didn't want to discuss why he still wore the sign of their commitment, not when he couldn't even explain it to himself.

She looked away and he could see a pulse beating at the base of her throat. He wanted to press his lips to the delicate skin there, feel for himself the effect he was having on her.

It was so rare for him to touch her outside the bedroom. After they'd established themselves as a couple, they had never bothered with such shows of romance. Why would they? Their marriage had never been about that.

Now though…now that he was staring into forever without her, now that he was looking at her, watching her body sway to the music, seeing her dress swirl around her feet, around his legs, a bright shock of crimson against the black suit pants, he regretted it.

He released his hold on her hand, tracing a line down her cheek, meeting her eyes. "How long has it been since we danced?"

Lucy looked away from Nico, trying to get a hold on her senses. They were currently galloping ahead of her like wild horses, her heartbeat keeping time with imaginary hoofbeats. How had she allowed herself to forget the effect he had on her?

She should have known that the moment he touched her she would be lost.

It had been that way from the beginning.

She remembered clearly just before they had announced their engagement how he had demanded they test their chemistry. He was not, he had said, marrying a woman whose bed he had no desire to be in. She had been angry then. Because in her mind passion had nothing to do with their arrangement. For all she cared, he could take mistresses.

At least, that had been her feeling just before his lips had touched hers.

From that moment she had known she would be his, and his alone. And that she would demand he be hers. That kiss had changed something in her, had opened up a well of deep longing she hadn't realized was there. He had made her aware in that moment of how much of life she had been missing pouring herself into her work at the exclusion of all else. Doing her very best to continue on the legacy her father hadn't been able to see through.

After his death when Lucy was nineteen, she had become obsessed with the idea of keeping things going. Of taking the company to the place her father had imagined it could go. But somewhere in all of that, in the midst of trying to live out someone else's dreams, she had lost pieces of herself. Had become hollow, incomplete. And Nico... Teaching her to want again... He had made her so painfully aware of it.

From there, it had been a slow descent into madness. Of becoming increasingly aware of that emptiness until she'd had to change something. Ironically, without Nico she never would have realized the emptiness was there. Ironic, because it was her feelings for him that made her so aware, that made it impossible to stay.

That made it so painful to leave.

Yes, she had told him in the beginning she had no need of love.

She had been a fool.

Because the moment his lips had touched hers five long years ago, she had realized that everything she believed about herself was a lie.

And on her wedding night she had discovered that not only did she desperately want love, craved it, but she wanted it from her husband.

The man who had vowed to stay with her in sickness and in health, for richer or poorer.

The man who had also vowed, after the wedding ceremony, once they were alone, that he would never, ever love her.

Memories of the past echoed through Nico as he twirled his wife around the dance floor. Strange that an action so foreign to them should conjure up memories. More than memories, there was a strange, hollow ache. Of memories that should have been.

He had not taken her dancing. They had danced at their wedding, as they had been expected to do. Once at a gala when they had been establishing their couple status with the public. But never since.

Regret lanced him, stealing his breath. This would be the last time they danced. He had not appreciated that before. Had not fully appreciated all of the things he would never do again with her once they had divorced.

Certainly, there would be other women. Of course there would be. He had not been a monk prior to his marriage, so it stood to reason he would not be after. And yet, the prospect did not fill him with excitement. Not in the least. He did not feel as if he had been unchained from a shackle. Rather, he felt as though he were walking back into a dungeon he had already been freed from once.

A strange feeling. Ridiculous.

And yet, he could not shake it off. Not now he had had it.

He tried to remember the last time they had made love. He had not been conscious of the fact it would be the last time. Her request for a divorce had come out of the blue, during the middle of the day. There had been no opportunity to say goodbye. No opportunity to cement the end of their relationship with a final coupling.

He could no longer let that stand. He could not endure it.

This was to be their last dance. And tonight, Christmas Eve, would be their last night together.

Nico Katsaros was a man who went after what he wanted. And right now he wanted to seduce his wife.

"Good thing we have the masks. We might have caused some gossip otherwise," Lucy said, her voice soft.

"Would that be the worst thing?"

"There would be no truth to the rumors."

"Is there no truth in this?" he asked, taking the opportunity to trace the lush outline of her ruby lips again, her warmth and softness beneath his fingertip a tease he could scarcely withstand.

"Attraction. But we've been down that road. It ends. I ended it."

"It does not end for two more nights. Tonight. We can have tonight."

"Nico…"

And suddenly, he was not content to simply touch her lips. He had to taste them as well.

With the music in the background promising with sincerity that the singer would be home for Christmas, Nico bent his head and kissed his wife.

And for the first time in six months, he did indeed feel as though he was home.

Surely, over the course of five years of marriage, Nico had kissed her thousands of times. But in this moment she forgot them all. She forgot everything but this. But his lips on hers, in this moment. Forgot everything except what a revelation this was.

She clung to him, curling her fingers around the collar of his suit jacket, holding him to her, afraid that this moment, this man, would disappear back into the ether if she let go for more than one second.

It was ridiculous to want to hang on, when she was the one who had decided they needed to let go. And yet, here she was. Hanging on to him as though he were the only thing keeping her afloat in the storm.

Don't do this to yourself again.

Her heart was screaming at her. Six months. She had spent six months trying to get over Nico Katsaros and now she was going to fall willingly back into his arms? Back into his bed? She knew how this would go. There was no twist ending awaiting her.

But she couldn't resist. She never could. No, not from that first kiss all the way until this one. She had never been able to resist.

"One last time," he said against her mouth, his voice rough. "Give me this. Please."

"Why?" she whispered.

"So that I know it is the last time."

"What do you mean?"

"You surprised me with the divorce. I am certain that you knew the last time we made love would be the last time. But I did not."

Her face heated. Because she did know. She had been so acutely aware that she was saying goodbye to him the night before he left for that last business trip. She had known that she would be giving him the divorce papers when he returned. But he had no way of knowing that.

She had known that last night that it was goodbye. And she had said it, with her body. Carried it with her even now.

"I didn't think you would care." She hadn't thought he would. Not for one second. She was surprised he hadn't replaced her in his bed already. She had never imagined she was special. She was just convenient.

"I care very much. And I am owed my goodbye."

She tried to squash the little bit of hope blooming in her chest. He cared about sex. He didn't care about her. His pride was likely wounded by her abandonment. Unsurprising, considering Nico was a very proud man.

And she wasn't nearly proud enough. Right now she felt needy, weak. Desperate for one more time.

"Then I'll give it to you. One last night."

He nodded once, his expression like stone. "One last night."

He broke their hold, his hand wrapping around hers as he led her from the dance floor. Every eye was on the masked couple as they broke through the crowd, moving quickly toward the lobby of the hotel.

Her heart was in her throat as they approached the front desk, and then, off to the left, she spotted a man in a suit. Tall, arresting.

Spencer Chatsfield.

Nico paused, then redirected their movements. "Hello, Mr. Chatsfield. We need a room for the night. Give us the best you have."

Spencer arched a brow, assessing them both, his expression carefully neutral. "Of course."

The moment Nico and Lucy were inside the elevator, the doors closed. Nico turned to her, pinning her against the wall, his hands on either side of her head. Restraint be damned. He had been nothing but patient. Nothing but restrained in the months since she had served him with divorce papers. Hadn't he given her everything she had demanded? Certainly, he had punished her by withholding her company from her, but she had broken her vows, and it was no less than she deserved.

Anger was once again penetrating the fog of lust that had descended over him. For a long time now, there had been only anger, blinding, white-hot anger. And now there was both. An intense need that was threatening to choke the life out of him combined with a kind of futile rage that he imagined one felt when they were watching the life's blood drain out of something precious. A kind of rage directed at the universe, a rage that had no recourse, no productivity. A rage that could fix nothing. A rage that could do nothing but simply be, filling up his entire being until he was driven by it, consumed by it.

He felt helpless in the face of it, and so, he dipped his head and consumed her. Poured all of it onto the woman who had caused it.

He broke the kiss, his lips still touching hers. "You have never done what I expected. You have never done what I asked."

She looked at him, glittering blue eyes filled with an anger that matched his own. "How can you say that? I was nothing but the perfect wife to you."

"You left me. And before that you tempted me. That was never a part of our bargain."

"I never tempted you. Temptation implies that it was something you wanted to resist. You demanded that I prove we have chemistry. And once we were married I was your business partner during the day and your whore at night. Nothing more. Never anything more. Don't you dare try and pretend I surprised you somehow. All I ever wanted was the business end of the arrangement. I never wanted this."

"You never wanted my kiss?"

"I never wanted to *need* it."

"And do you need it? Have you spent nights as I have? Aching, alone, desperate for something you know you can only have with the one person you can never touch again?"

She looked down. "I don't—"

He gripped her chin and forced her to look up at him. "Speak to me. Not to the floor."

"Yes," she said.

"I promise you one thing. After tonight you will burn for me forever."

By the time she and Nico entered the hotel room, she was shaking. His words were echoing in her mind.

After tonight you will burn for me forever.

She feared it was true. Because if the past few months were any indicator, she would never forget what it was like to be touched by him, kissed by him. She had a feeling that even if she went forward with life, filling up those empty spaces as best she could, there would always be one left vacant. Hollow. A space that could only ever be filled by Nico.

Nico sat on the edge of the mattress, leaning back, his thighs spread, the outline of his arousal clearly visible through his dark dress pants. Yes, she wanted him. Yes, she was going to have this. Even if it did make her burn. Forever and ever after. It would be worth it.

Just have him look at her like this again. To have him touch her again.

She reached up, ready to untie the mask that concealed part of her face.

"Leave it," he said, his words clipped, hard.

She lowered her hands. "And are you leaving yours?" she asked, looking at the slash of black leather still resting over his eyes.

"There is a certain appeal to it, don't you think? The opportunity to come together as strangers again. Perhaps we will learn new things, rather than simply assuming we already know them?"

She clung to part of his words, held them close to her chest. Strangers. Maybe if she could think of him as a stranger, this wouldn't hurt quite so much. Maybe she could get what she wanted from this without the pain.

She grabbed hold of the zipper tab on her dress, and slowly began to lower it. Letting her gown fall loose, leaving her standing there bare before her husband.

Nico took in the sight of his wife's body, her every delicious curve bared for his inspection. Only two things remained. Black panties that scarcely concealed anything, rather framing the part of herself he was most interested in. And the mask, a brilliant gold against her skin. His gift, unwrapped in all her glory.

Dark curls cascaded over her shoulders, her lips a crimson temptation.

He recalled the first time he had seen his wife, in her prim little business suits. He could never have imagined they would end up here. About to make love in a hotel room, wearing masks. On the brink of divorce.

He had a moment of feeling as though he were in someone else's life. A life not his own.

He'd had this woman. His wife. And he had somehow let her escape. Nico Katsaros, who failed at nothing. Who had dragged himself up from the bottom rung of society to the very top. And yet, it had not been enough. It had not been enough to keep his wife with him.

Had he not offered her everything? Money, security for her business, sex.

Somehow, as far as this woman was concerned, he was still not enough. He hated that feeling. Loathed it more than anything else on earth. He had spent all of his life being treated as though he was not enough, as though he was deficient because of his birth.

She had no right to treat him that way. Not now. No one did. He owned the world.

But you do not own her.

He gritted his teeth against that reminder. Perhaps not. Not in the grand scheme of things. But tonight he did.

"Come to me, Lucy. Give yourself to me," he said, each word a struggle.

She obeyed, moving nearer to him, pressing her knee into the mattress beside his thigh. "I thought we were strangers tonight?"

"If you please." He ran his thumb along the edge of her mask, then stretched up to kiss her mouth. "Show me what you like."

Lucy was shaking, her hands aching to touch, her body hollow with the need to be possessed by him. It was terrifying to need like this. This was why she had consented to marry Nico in the first place to save her father's ailing company. Because as far as she was concerned, a convenient marriage was the safest route to take. She didn't want to love, not again.

Everyone in her life she had loved, she had lost. Her mother had left before she was born, her father died far too soon…

She had never wanted to submit herself to that kind of pain again. That risk of loss.

It was why there had been no other men before Nico. She had avoided relationships, avoided attachments. She had imagined it would be easy to steer clear of emotional strings with a man like Nico. A man whose foundation was set upon business, his personal life built upon the sand, ever shifting and reshaping. He'd had a reputation as quite the playboy prior to their marriage. The sort of man women linked themselves to for an evening, but no more.

Foolish girl she had been, she had figured she would simply do the same. Connect herself physically with no emotional repercussions.

But she had been wrong. So very wrong.

He was right—she was keeping secrets from him. But it hadn't started that way.

Something had changed in her over the course of their marriage, taking root in her soul. Building, growing, until it had been almost impossible to hold back anymore. She had tried to deny it, not even allowing herself to think the words.

But they were there. Echoing through her all the same.

And as Nico rested his hand on her hip, dark eyes intent on her, she let them flow through her for the first time. Let her mind form them fully.

She had her secrets. But they were not the sorts of secrets he imagined.

Her deepest secret was that she had fallen in love with her husband.

Nico was thankful they were wearing the masks. Otherwise, he knew Lucy would be able to see the raw hunger on his face. Would be able to see just how close he was to losing control.

He moved his palm up from her hip, along the elegant curve of her waist, to the full, brilliant temptation of her breasts. A mere mask could never make them strangers, though he appreciated the small barrier it provided. Still, had he been wearing a blindfold he would've known it was her. Would have known the particular softness of her skin, the exact slope of the indent of her waist, just where her breasts grew fuller.

He knew her body as well as he knew his own.

This was the last time.

That was the agreement.

Her hands went to his tie, delicate fingers slipping the silk through the knot. He had forgotten the simple pleasure of having her undress him. The beauty in anticipating their coming together. Before their marriage he had been with countless women, but from the moment his lips had touched hers, he had never wanted another.

Slowly, she slipped her fingertips inside his shirt, her palm resting over his raging heartbeat.

He lifted his gaze from her beautiful body to her eyes. She was trying to hide too. Trying to use the mask to conceal how she felt in the intensity of this moment.

He raised his own hand, placed it over hers, trapping it against his skin. Then he closed the distance between them and kissed her.

Lucy made quick work of her husband's clothes, repeating actions she had carried out hundreds of times before. But this was different. Final. It made her ache.

She drank in the sight of him. His broad shoulders and chest, sprinkled with just the right amount of chest hair. His well-defined abs that shifted and rippled with each indrawn breath. And of course, the most male part of him, the part of him that she was desperate for now.

She memorized every detail. The flex of his thighs, the way his fingers curled around the bedspread, the gold wedding band he still wore bright against his dark skin, the tendons in the backs of his hands standing out as he fought to anchor himself to the bed.

She straddled his lap, kissing him deeply as she pressed her breasts against him. It was sexual, there was no denying it, but there was also something deeply emotional about being close to him like this again. Being skin to skin.

She had, after years of it, taken such intimacy for granted. Had been certain it hadn't been intimacy at all. But now that she had been living without him, she knew that hadn't been true. Recognized that there had been more emotion when they'd touched than she had begun to imagine. Empty, she had allowed herself to believe it was empty.

Now she felt that evaluation may have been unfair.

"Have you continued to take your contraceptive pill?" he asked, his voice rough, strained.

He was as near the edge as she was, and she found it immensely gratifying.

She nodded, because speech was beyond. His mouth went slightly slack, abject relief visible on his face even with some of his features obscured by the mask.

He wrapped his arm around her waist, moving his hand down to cup her rear, and at the same time sweeping her panties to the side. She shifted her position, and allowed him to slide deep inside of her.

Tears stung the backs of her eyes, and she shut them tight to try to keep them back.

How had she ever thought this was empty?

This was the last time. And she feared that without Nico, she would never be anything but empty ever again.

He was surrounded by her, lost in her. The feel of her, the scent of her. He reached up, sifting his fingers through her silky curtain of dark curls, relishing the sensation. He flexed his hips, sliding deeper inside the damp heat of her body.

He had thought their first time, five years ago, was powerful. But it was nothing in comparison to this. Because in their first time had been the promise of forever, while this was the promise of an end. And with that came the desperation to make it count, to make it last. To make sure she would burn, forever.

Because he would.

He grabbed hold of her bottom, moving into a standing position, wrapping her legs around his waist, keeping himself buried deep inside of her. He turned and lowered her back to the bed, reversing their positions and thrusting down inside of her.

He was as deep in her as he could possibly get, and it wasn't enough. It would never be enough.

She gasped, arching against him, and he captured the

sound with his mouth, kissing her as he allowed himself to get lost in the rhythm of their bodies. Lost in her.

Soon, too soon, his climax rushed up to meet him, overtaking him like a savage beast, grabbing him by the throat and shaking him hard, leaving pleasure to bleed out through his body in an unstoppable tide. He gritted his teeth and thrust into her one last time, grinding against the bundle of nerves at the apex of her thighs, holding position until she made the sweet familiar sound of release, her internal muscles tightening around him.

He didn't move, not for a long while. Her red lips parted, a long sigh escaping.

And then a single tear tracked from beneath her golden mask and slid down her cheek, leaving a dark blot on the pillowcase.

"Lucy?" he asked, moving away from her.

She shook her head. "No. No names. Please. Please let's be strangers."

Lucy was gasping for breath, a haze of pleasure tangling with the sharp, keen clarity of what she had just done. Of the fact that it was over.

He started to get up, as was his routine after they made love. For all five years of their marriage, they would make love and he would leave, go back to his own room, leave her there with nothing more than his scent on her pillow to keep her company as her sheets cooled.

She couldn't stand that right now. Just this once, she needed him to stay.

"Don't go."

He paused. "But you're upset."

"No. Yes," she said, laughing slightly while she wiped

the moisture from her cheeks. "I don't know what I am. But I don't want to be alone."

"You like to be left alone. After we…"

"What made you think that?"

"You prize your space, Lucy. I have always tried to respect that. You made it very plain when we were first married that you wanted to sleep alone."

His words hit her like a brick. They weren't wrong. She had made a very big deal about wanting to preserve her space. But that was before they were married. Certainly before they had shared years of intimacy. Surely, he must have known that she would want him to stay.

"I didn't always want space," she said.

"When? When did it change?"

She knew when. But she didn't want to tell him.

"We were strangers when we first married. Of course, after we got to know each other. After it was more than just physical… I suppose I never told you."

"No."

"I wished you would stay." So much easier to tell him these things while she was wearing the mask. While she was pretending they were just strangers, talking. Yes, they were talking about a shared past, but somehow the game, the idea, allowed her the distance she needed to speak to him without falling apart.

"I would have liked that," he said, his voice rough.

"We kept too many secrets."

Dark eyes met hers, and he moved nearer to her again. "Did we? What were yours? Tell me your secrets, *agape*."

Nico watched the pulse beat hard at the base of her neck, watched as the delicate color leached from her cheeks.

She was so beautiful. He had always thought so. But he didn't know if he had ever *felt* it.

He felt it now. Echoing in his soul, reverberating down deep in his bones. The kind of beauty you didn't just witness, but the kind that took up residence inside you. Changed you. How had he been blind to it until he had lost it?

"You don't want to know about me," she said, her voice soft.

"There will never be another chance for me to learn. And we are just strangers. So tell me. Tell me who you are. Then, when we leave here, perhaps we will not be strangers. Though, we will not meet again," he said.

"You know everything there is to know about me."

"No, I don't. Because we are strangers. Talk to me like I am a stranger, and not your husband. And I daresay I will learn more in that conversation than any we have had in the past five years." He didn't know why he was making the demand, didn't know why it suddenly seemed so important. Only that it did.

She shifted her position, rolling to her side, and he watched her breasts move with her. Completely captivated, but not only by her body—by the words she would speak next. "All right. You know my mother left. And that it was just me and my father. And I wanted... I wanted so badly to please him. And I did. I poured everything that I was into learning about Kennewick, into helping him with ideas. I wanted to be involved in it so that we would have something in common. And he loved sharing all of that with me. And then he died. And Kennewick was all I had. By the time you and I met... I felt as though everything that I had ever cared about I was destined to lose. So that's why I couldn't find someone to be my maid of honor at the wedding. And that's why there were no men before you. Because earning the love of the only family member I had left meant pouring everything into the company. And I did love Kennewick. But you can love a business, and you can love the money it brings in. But it can never love you back." She took a deep breath. "Finally, I realized that. I realized that no amount of pouring into it would replicate the love I had lost when my father died. And so, I decided I was tired of pouring in and getting nothing back. I decided I was tired of being empty."

"You felt… Empty? Even when you were with me?"

She lifted a bare shoulder. "Sometimes being skin to skin with someone and knowing they don't care for you is even more devastating than simply being alone." She pushed herself into a sitting position, drawing her knees up to her chest. "Now…tell me your secrets."

Lucy watched, waited to see if he would turn away from her, or if he would share. She wanted him to tell her, wanted to tear down that wall that he kept between himself and the world, himself and her, and finally understand the man she had shared her life with for half a decade. Of course, it wasn't fair. Because she had talked of familial love, and manufacturing companies, and never once spoken of the fact that what had truly left her feeling empty was loving him when she knew he didn't love her back.

"I was the bastard son of a poor woman. I worked hard, got straight A's in school, got scholarships, worked my way from the ground up at one of the largest national conglomerates… But you can find all this out by reading my bio."

"But we are sharing. As though we're strangers," she said. "What inspired you to work hard? What inspired you to change?"

There was a slight pause. "I saw opulence all around me every day, and yet I was not allowed to partake in it. I vowed that I would have my own piece of that opulence someday. I was so tired of being denied."

It was easy then, to imagine him as a small boy, surrounded by the luxuries of the world while constantly being told they were off-limits. How confusing it must have been.

"You must be proud. Of everything you have achieved."

"Typically. Typically, I am. And yet, I find myself being denied again. I don't like it, Lucy. I don't like it one bit."

"What have you been denied?"

His dark eyes blazed into hers. "You."

Her heart leaped against her breastbone. "Find another wife. It won't be difficult for you."

"But it's you that I want. I want you."

"Why? Because I matter? Because you're still a small boy throwing a tantrum over the things you can't have?"

A feral growl escaped his lips, and she found herself pinned against the mattress, Nico above her, his expression fierce. And for the first time that night, he reached up and tore off the mask.

"Am I a boy? I think not. Perhaps you need me to show you again that I am in fact very much a man."

"Why would you need to show me?" she asked, desperation pouring through her. "Why should you care?"

"Do not forget that you are the one who demanded

to divorce, *agape*. Not me. I did not want this. I never wanted it."

"Why?" she asked, ferocity lacing her tone. "You haven't given me a satisfactory answer to my question."

He growled, flexing his hips, giving her a taste of his growing arousal, and in spite of herself, her body responded. "Is this not answer enough?"

"No. You have always acted like it should be enough. It isn't enough."

"Why not? I gave you my name. I gave you my money. I saved your failing business. I gave you my home. A place in my bed. And you reject me. You tell me I'm not enough. I made vows to you, and still I am not enough."

"Because you didn't give me what I wanted."

"You have never told me what you wanted," he said, desperation filling his tone now, matching her own. "You didn't tell me you wanted to share my bed all night. You didn't tell me you wanted to share a room. You kept these things from me, and then you punished me for not guessing what you never spoke out loud."

There was no response she could give to that. Because he was right. She had never told him what she wanted. Had never told him what she felt, that she was empty, that she was desperate for more from him. She hadn't told him that she loved him. She had been consumed with protecting herself, with preventing another loss. So she had run, not realizing the fatal flaw in her plan. She already loved him, so whether or not she told him, whether or not she ever gave him the chance to reject her, she would lose him if she ran.

But she didn't know if she was brave enough to stay. Didn't know if she was brave enough to speak those words to him, to watch his face change. To one of horror, of pity. He didn't want love; he had stated it plainly. Had told her explicitly after their wedding that theirs would never be a union held together by emotion.

So she had believed him.

What you wanted changed. Perhaps what he wanted has changed too. But you will never know, because you are a coward.

It was true. She was.

And it had to stop.

She curled her fingers around her mask and pulled it away. And they were Nico and Lucy again. There was no more hiding. She refused to hide anymore.

"I still haven't told you my last secret."

Nico looked down at his wife, her eyes glittering with emotion, and he felt his rage drain away. He moved away from her, pushing himself into a sitting position and forking his fingers through his hair. "I'm sorry, Lucy."

He heard the rustle of the covers as she sat up, felt the light touch of her fingertips against his shoulder. "Do you want to hear my secret?"

His chest seized up tight. "Is it fair to say that I'm not sure?"

"I suppose so. Since I'm not sure I want to tell it. But I realized that all of the silence between us is what broke things. So I doubt there's anything I could say now that would make it worse."

"We are getting divorced the day after tomorrow. It doesn't get worse than that."

She laughed softly, her breath fanning over his bare skin. "I suppose so." Still, she said nothing. She only moved nearer to him, pressed her body against him, holding him.

"You're stalling, *agape*."

"You always call me that," she said, her voice soft.

"I suppose I do."

"From the beginning. You've always called me that."

Discomfort crawled over his skin. "Yes. It is a common endearment."

"It means *love*."

"I'm well aware of the meaning."

"I used to find it slightly annoying. I mean at first. Because it was all a charade, and neither you nor I were pretending to have any finer feelings. But one day…one day you said it and everything sort of slowed down. And I realized that whether or not you meant anything when you called me that it meant something to me. Because, Nico, I love you."

Heat and cold rushed through Nico's body, a reaction he could not have anticipated.

But then, his wife's words were nothing he could have ever anticipated. She loved him? And she was telling him this two nights before their divorce was final.

He turned to look at the clock. After midnight. Not even two nights until their divorce was final. It was Christmas now.

He stood, collecting his clothes and putting them on as quickly as possible. He was aware of Lucy watching him, but he didn't look at her. He couldn't look at her. He was too lost in the feelings riding through him. Anger. Pain. But most of all, fear.

It was the fear that won.

"Our last night together has come to an end," he said, keeping his eyes fixed on a place on the wall behind her. "Merry Christmas, Lucy."

And then he turned and walked out the door.

* * *

It was a truly vile Christmas, thank you very much. No matter how resolutely the radio played music proclaiming it a merry one, Lucy simply couldn't feel it.

She had done it. She had told him. Confessed all, and he had rejected her. No, he had not even had the decency to reject her. He had simply walked out. With nary anything but a season's greeting.

She should feel vindicated. Obviously, she had been right asking for the divorce. Obviously, no amount, or lack, of communication could have possibly altered the course of their relationship. She had changed, what she wanted had changed, but what he wanted hadn't.

Certainly, he had been more than willing to have sex with her, but that was no indication of any finer feelings. Typical.

She took a sip of wine, then set her glass back down on the sideboard in the living room. The crystal made contact with the wood surface with a resounding click, echoing against the walls of her family home. Highlighting the fact that she was truly alone.

Here she was, living the exact thing she had been afraid of. Loving again. Losing it again.

The only positive thing she could say was that she was living. For now, she would take it.

The doorbell rang, and she crossed the expansive living area, heading toward the entry. If it was carolers, she could not promise she wouldn't throw them in a snowbank. She wasn't feeling particularly cheered, and she didn't really want anyone to try.

She paused at the door and looked through the security glass. And then her heart stopped. There were no Dickensian street urchins, no carolers of any kind.

It was Nico.

She opened the door to the town house, her sadness suddenly washed away by a torrent of anger. "What do you want? You didn't hurt me enough last night? Have you also come to step on my toe? Get a red wine stain on the cream-colored rug? Or perhaps something else similarly damaging?"

"No," he said, his voice ragged. For the first time, she paused and looked at him, really looked. And she noticed he appeared as though he had not slept since he had left her in the hotel room. "I came here because I have one more secret to tell you."

The last time Nico had felt so nervous, he had knocked over a vase in the hallowed halls of the home his mother had worked in. He had known then, though he had been only a child, that he had broken something priceless. That there would be no fixing it. That the only way out would be if those he had wronged forgave his debt, because there was no way he could pay it.

It was the same as this moment. He had broken something last night. Perhaps he had been steadily breaking it over the past five years. He wasn't sure there was any way to fix it. And so, instead he would ask for forgiveness. And offer something in return.

"Tell me," Lucy said, her voice thin.

"I hated Christmas as a child. It was so happy and warm. It was everything I was not. A display of all I could not have. It made me want. It made me feel. It made me ache. To be tantalized by all that you cannot have from your very earliest memory… There was a point where I decided I would never do that again. I would no longer want—I would have. And I would do what needed to be done to obtain the means to make it possible. Then I met you. And I... I acquired you. As I have done many things in the past."

"I'm not certain I find that flattering."

"It isn't. Simply the reasoning of a frightened man." He drew a deep breath. "We were married for five years. And I never once brought a Christmas tree or anything festive at all into our house, did I?"

"No," she said.

"It is because I didn't want to ache anymore. Reminders of the past...of that longing... They only made me ache and so I kept them away. But I couldn't stop that pain forever."

"You couldn't?"

"No. Because of you. You are my Christmas, Lucy Kennewick."

"I'm your what?"

"You are my Christmas. Being near you, so close to you, and yet not having you made me ache. So I pretended I didn't need you. I pretended you weren't important. When in truth all I really wanted was one moment of the warmth, of the happiness, I knew I could find in you." He cleared his throat. "But I was afraid. Afraid of wanting something I might not be able to have. You were right, in many ways. I am just a boy afraid of being denied."

Lucy felt as though her heart was going to explode. She stepped out the door, wrapping her arms around Nico, squeezing her eyes shut tight. "Oh, Nico. You don't have to be afraid of me. You don't have to be afraid of not having me."

"When you asked for your divorce... I told myself I hated you. Because yet again I was being denied. So I decided I wouldn't think of you. I wouldn't remember you. I wouldn't want you. Because it was better than the pain." He looked away. "Of course… I could not let go entirely. It's why I wore the ring still. Because I didn't want it to be over, no matter what I told myself."

"I hurt you? Believe me when I tell you I had no clue I possessed the power to hurt you."

He drew back slightly, his dark eyes trained on hers. "I didn't know either. Because I worked so hard to ensure that nothing did. But you…you got beneath my defenses. You were so unexpected. A virgin in business suits who wanted a marriage of convenience. Why should I ever think I would have to protect my heart from such a creature?"

She frowned. "I am not a creature."

He leaned in and kissed her lips lightly. "Of course not."

"So what do you…? I mean… How do you feel about Christmas now?" she asked, her heart thundering heavily.

"I assume by Christmas you mean you."

"That is the metaphor."

A smile curved his lips. "Aren't you going to invite me in?"

Nico had spent the whole night wandering the city feeling tortured. Feeling as though his heart had been ripped straight out of his chest and hung up on a tree in Rockefeller Center as a macabre ornament.

And then he had asked himself what the hell he was doing, wandering the city streets in the cold when he could be with his wife. When there was a woman who loved him. A woman he knew beyond a shadow of a doubt he wanted to spend the rest of his life with.

So, he had come to her.

"I would invite you in," she said, blocking the door with her petite frame. "But there are Christmas decorations in there. And I'm not sure yet how you feel about those."

"I love them," he said, the words rough, torn from him.

Her lips went slack, rounded into an O. "You do?"

"Yes."

"Why...why did you never tell Christmas? And why did you let Christmas almost divorce you? And why did you walk out of the hotel room without saying anything when Christmas confessed its true feelings?"

"Because," he said, tugging Lucy into his arms and kissing her hard. "Because I am little more than a frightened boy. I had aspirations. I wanted things. But, Lucy, that's nothing compared to risking your heart. I didn't want to let anything or anyone hurt me, ever again. I married you because you were safe. But then it turned out you weren't. So I kept you at a distance and...and then you left me. Lucy, these past six months without you have been hell."

"They have been," she said. "I mean, for me too. Without you."

"I know I don't ever want to lose you again. And I know that means investing more than I have. I know that means giving. I know that means opening up. It means risking pain."

"But healing too," she said, tears filling her eyes. "And happiness. And love. Lots of love."

He kissed her again. "I know. It's worth the risk. And now you know my secrets. If I ever close up, if I ever turn away..."

"I'll ask you why. And you do the same for me."

"I promise."

"I love you, Nico."

His heart expanded in his chest. "I love you too, Lucy. Stay my wife. Please."

"I will." She kissed him again and he looked beyond her, through the door and at the house inside. He could see a Christmas tree, lights twinkling everywhere. And he knew for a fact Christmas would never again be a promise not kept.

It would be, for him, the ultimate symbol of vows honored.

"Now maybe you should come inside," she said, a smile on her face. "I have a present for you that you might want to unwrap."

* * * * *

COMING NEXT MONTH FROM

HARLEQUIN

Presents®

Available December 15, 2015

#3393 THE QUEEN'S NEW YEAR SECRET

Princes of Petras

by Maisey Yates

The fairy tale is over for all of Petras when Queen Tabitha—refusing to live in a loveless marriage—asks her husband for a divorce. But anger erupts into passion, and when Tabitha flees the palace she's carrying King Kairos's heir!

#3394 THE COST OF THE FORBIDDEN

Irresistible Russian Tycoons

by Carol Marinelli

Ruthless Sev Derzhavin is master of getting whatever—and whomever—he wants. He's never been refused before, so when his personal assistant Naomi resigns, Sev can't resist the challenge of *enticing* the beautiful brunette to stay.

#3395 THESEUS DISCOVERS HIS HEIR

The Kalliakis Crown

by Michelle Smart

Stunning Joanne Brooks's arrival on Agon has given the royal family more than they bargained for...she's the mother of Prince Theseus's secret love child! How will she react now that the commanding prince wants to claim his heir *and* his bride?

#3396 NEW YEAR AT THE BOSS'S BIDDING

by Rachael Thomas

Tilly Rogers is thrilled to be offered a prestigious contract for billionaire Xavier Moretti's New Year's Eve party—until she ends up snowbound alone with her boss! The notorious playboy makes it his resolution to seduce virgin Tilly...

HPCNM1215RA

#3397 AWAKENING THE RAVENSDALE HEIRESS
The Ravensdale Scandals
by Melanie Milburne

Miranda Ravensdale's first love ended in tragedy, so she vowed to bury her heart with the memories. No man has broken through her facade—until billionaire Leandro Allegretti! Leandro plans to coax her dormant sensuality into life, kiss by seductive kiss...

#3398 WEARING THE DE ANGELIS RING
The Italian Titans
by Cathy Williams

Tycoon Theo De Angelis lives by his own rules...until a family debt forces him into matrimony! Beautiful, inexperienced Alexa Caldini is determined to impose ground rules on their inconvenient arrangement, but how long before Alexa's rules go up in smoke?

#3399 THE MARRIAGE HE MUST KEEP
The Wrong Heirs
by Dani Collins

Alessandro Ferrante was pleasantly surprised to discover passion in his convenient marriage to shy heiress Octavia. But when their fragile union is tested, Alessandro *must* seduce his wife again and ensure Octavia—and his child—are his forever!

#3400 MISTRESS OF HIS REVENGE
Bought by the Brazilian
by Chantelle Shaw

Cruz Delgado is the renowned owner of a diamond empire—and aristocratic Sabrina Bancroft is the *only* woman ever to have walked away from the tempting tycoon. When Cruz sees a chance, he takes his revenge...by making her his mistress!

REQUEST YOUR FREE BOOKS!

HARLEQUIN

Presents®

2 FREE NOVELS PLUS
2 FREE GIFTS!

PASSION · SEDUCTION · GUARANTEED

YES! Please send me 2 FREE Harlequin Presents® novels and my 2 FREE gifts (gifts are worth about $10). After receiving them, if I don't wish to receive any more books, I can return the shipping statement marked "cancel." If I don't cancel, I will receive 6 brand-new novels every month and be billed just $4.30 per book in the U.S. or $5.24 per book in Canada. That's a saving of at least 13% off the cover price! It's quite a bargain! Shipping and handling is just 50¢ per book in the U.S. and 75¢ per book in Canada.* I understand that accepting the 2 free books and gifts places me under no obligation to buy anything. I can always return a shipment and cancel at any time. Even if I never buy another book, the two free books and gifts are mine to keep forever.

106/306 HDN GHRP

Name	(PLEASE PRINT)

Address		Apt. #

City	State/Prov.	Zip/Postal Code

Signature (if under 18, a parent or guardian must sign)

Mail to the **Reader Service:**
IN U.S.A.: P.O. Box 1867, Buffalo, NY 14240-1867
IN CANADA: P.O. Box 609, Fort Erie, Ontario L2A 5X3

**Are you a current subscriber to Harlequin Presents® books
and want to receive the larger-print edition?
Call 1-800-873-8635 or visit www.ReaderService.com.**

* Terms and prices subject to change without notice. Prices do not include applicable taxes. Sales tax applicable in N.Y. Canadian residents will be charged applicable taxes. Offer not valid in Quebec. This offer is limited to one order per household. Not valid for current subscribers to Harlequin Presents books. All orders subject to credit approval. Credit or debit balances in a customer's account(s) may be offset by any other outstanding balance owed by or to the customer. Please allow 4 to 6 weeks for delivery. Offer available while quantities last.

Your Privacy—The Reader Service is committed to protecting your privacy. Our Privacy Policy is available online at www.ReaderService.com or upon request from the Reader Service.

We make a portion of our mailing list available to reputable third parties that offer products we believe may interest you. If you prefer that we not exchange your name with third parties, or if you wish to clarify or modify your communication preferences, please visit us at www.ReaderService.com/consumerschoice or write to us at Reader Service Preference Service, P.O. Box 9062, Buffalo, NY 14240-9062. Include your complete name and address.

HP15

"I don't think we've ever…really been alone before."

"We are very often alone," he said, frowning.

"In a palace filled with hundreds, in a building other people live in."

"I have never kidnapped you before, either. You've also never been pregnant with my baby. Oh, yes, and we have never been on the brink of divorce. So, a season of firsts. How nice to add this to the list."

She stood up, stretching out her stiff muscles. "Where exactly do you get off being angry at me? We are here because of you."

"I'm angry with you because this divorce is happening at your demand."

"Had I not demanded we divorce, I wouldn't be pregnant."

"Had you not frozen me out of your bed, perhaps you would have been pregnant a couple of months sooner."

She gritted her teeth, reckless heat pouring through her veins. "How dare you?" She advanced on him, and he wrapped his arm around her waist, pulling her close. "Don't."

Her protest was cut off by the press of his mouth against hers, hot and uncompromising, his tongue staking a claim as he took her deep, hard. She had no idea where these kinds of kisses had come from. Who this man was. This man who would spirit her away to a private island. Who kissed her like he was a dying man and her lips held his salvation.

He kissed her neck, down to her collarbone, retracing that same path with the tip of his tongue. She found herself tearing at his shirt, her heart thundering hard, every fiber of her being desperate to have him. Desperate to have him inside her again. Like that night in his office. That night when the promise that had been broken on their wedding night was finally fulfilled.

Don't miss
THE QUEEN'S NEW YEAR SECRET by Maisey Yates,
available January 2016 wherever
Harlequin Presents® books and ebooks are sold.

www.Harlequin.com

HARLEQUIN
Presents®

Kidnapped by her king!

The fairy tale is over for all of Petras when Queen Tabitha—refusing to live in a loveless marriage—asks her husband for a divorce. But anger erupts into passion, and when Tabitha flees the palace she's carrying King Kairos's heir!

SAVE $1.00

on the purchase of THE QUEEN'S NEW YEAR SECRET by Maisey Yates {available Dec. 15, 2015} or any other Harlequin Presents® book.

Redeemable at participating outlets in the U.S. and Canada only. Not redeemable at Barnes & Noble stores. Limit one coupon per customer.

COUPON EXPIRES JAN. 4, 2016

Available wherever books are sold, including most bookstores, supermarkets, drugstores and discount stores.

www.Harlequin.com

HARLEQUIN

Presents®

Don't miss Rachael Thomas's thrilling new
temptation-filled story, as a snowbound New Year's Eve
explodes into a night of forbidden passion with the boss!

Jilted bride Tilly Rogers is thrilled to be offered a
prestigious catering contract for billionaire
Xavier Moretti's New Year's Eve party…until she ends
up snowbound and at her boss's bidding!

It's the end of the year *and* the end of Tilly's
contract—leaving Xavier free to seduce her!
Hardly shy of a challenge, this notorious playboy
makes it his resolution to have virgin Tilly crumbling
under his experienced touch.

Find out what happens next in

NEW YEAR AT THE BOSS'S BIDDING

January 2016

Stay Connected:

Harlequin.com

iHeartPresents.com

f /HarlequinBooks

t @HarlequinBooks

p /HarlequinBooks

HP13402